With a broadsword in his hand, von Schlichten fought his way

toward the throne. There Firkked waited, a sword in one of his upper hands, his Spear of State in the other, and a dagger in each lower hand. Von Schlichten fought on, trying not to think of the absurdity of a man of the Sixth Century A.E., the representative of a civilized Chartered Company, dueling to the death with a barbarian king for a throne he had promised to another barbarian...or of what could happen on Uller if he allowed this four-armed monstrosity to kill him!

Ace Science Fiction Books by H. Beam Piper

Introduction to
ULLER UPRISING

by John F. Carr

With the publication of this novel, *Uller Uprising*, all of H. Beam Piper's previously published science fiction is now available in Ace editions. *Uller Uprising* was first published in 1952 in a Twayne Science Fiction Triplet—a hardbound collection of three thematically connected novels. (The other two were Judith Merril's *Daughters of Earth* and Fletcher Pratt's *The Long View*.) A year later it appeared in the February and March issues of *Space Science Fiction*, edited by Lester Del Rey.

The magazine version, which was abridged by about a third, was believed by many bibliographers to be the only version—and as a novella it was too short for book publication. The Twayne version had a small print run and is so scarce that few people have seen it. Those bibliographers who knew of its existence assumed that both versions of *Uller* were the same. It was through a telephone conversation with Charles N. Brown, publisher of *Locus* and correspondent with Piper, that I learned about the Twayne edition and its greater length. Brown allowed me to photocopy his original, for which we owe him a debt of thanks; because the Twayne version is not only novel length, but far better than the shorter one that appeared in *Space Science Fiction*.

Probably the most surprising and interesting thing about the Twayne edition is the essay that forms the introduction to that volume, and is reprinted here. The essay is by Dr. John D. Clark, an eminent scientist of the fourties and fifties and one of the discoverers of sulfa, the first "miracle drug." It describes in great detail the planetary system of the star Beta Hydri, and gives the names of those planets: Uller and Niflheim. A publisher's note states that Clark's essay was written first, and given to the contributors as background material for a novel they would then write.

The fans of H. Beam Piper seem to owe a great debt to Dr. Clark. *Uller Uprising* became the foundation of Piper's monumental Terro-Human Future History; the first story where we encounter the Terran Federation. In it we learn about Odin, the planet that will one day be the capital of the First Galactic Empire; and humble Niflheim, which in more decadent times will become a common expletive, a word meaning hell. This is also where Piper introduced and explained the Atomic Era dating system (A.E.). *Uller Uprising* is set in the early years of the Terran Federation's expansion and exploration, an epoch of great vitality. In "The Edge of the Knife" Piper compares this time of discovery to the Spanish conquest of the Americas. This feeling of vigor and unlimited possibilities runs through all the early Federation stories: *Uller Uprising,* "Omnilingual," "Naudsonce," "When in the Course—," and, to a lesser degree, in the late Federation novels, *Little Fuzzy, Fuzzy Sapiens,* and *Fuzzies and Other People*. (See *Federation* by H. Beam Piper for a good overview of this period.)

In these stories we see Terro-Humans at their best and at their worst: Individual heroism and bravery in the face of grave danger in *Uller Uprising;* Federation law and justice in *Little Fuzzy* and its sequels; and, in "Omnilingual" and "Naudsonce," the spirit of science and rational inquiry. Yet we also see colonial exploitation and subjugation in *Uller Uprising* and "Oomphel in the Sky," the greed and corruption of Chartered land companies in *Little Fuzzy,* and political corruption in *Four-Day Planet.* These stories are about a living Terro-Human culture, not a utopia.

It was Piper's attention to historical realism and his use of actual historical models that have helped his work to pass the test of time and have led to his becoming the favorite of a new generation of readers more than twenty-five years after his death.

Uller Uprising is the story of a confrontation between a human overlord and alien servants, with an ironic twist at the end. Like most of Piper's best work, *Uller Uprising* is modeled after an actual event in human history; in this case the Sepoy Mutiny (a Bengal uprising in British-held India brought about when rumors were spread to native soldiers that cartridges being issued by the British were coated with animal fat. The rebellion quickly spread throughout India and led to the massacre of the British Colony at Cawnpore.). Piper's novel is not a mere retelling of the Indian Mutiny, but rather an analysis of an historical event applied to a similar situation in the far future.

Like many philosophers and social theorists before him, Piper attempted to chart the progress of humankind; unlike most, however, he did not envision or try to create a system of ethics that would end all of humanity's problems. The best he could offer was his model of the self-reliant man: The man who "actually knows what has to be done and how to do it, and he's going to go right ahead and do it, without holding a dozen conferences and round-table discussions and giving everybody a fair and equal chance to foul things up for him."

Piper brought his own ideas and judgments about society and history into all of his work, but they appear most clearly in his Terro-Human Future History. While not everyone will agree with Piper's theories they give his work a bite that most popular fiction lacks. One cannot read Piper complacently. And one can often find a wry insight sandwiched in between the blood and thunder.

Other future histories may span more centuries or better illuminate the highlights of several decades, but until a rival is created with more historical depth and attention to detail, H. Beam Piper's Terro-Human Future History will stand as the Bayeux Tapestry of science fiction histories.

In many ways—certainly during his lifetime—Piper was the most underrated of the John W. Campbell's "Astounding" writers. He was probably also the most Campbellian; his *self-reliant man* is almost a mirror image of Campbell's "Citizen."

Piper died a bitter man, a failure in his own mind; shortly before his death he believed he could no longer earn a living as a writer without charity from his friends or the state.

Now he's the cornerstone of Ace Books. Had he lived long enough to finish another half dozen books, he would have been among the sf greats of the sixties. . . .

But maybe he does know, after all. Jerry Pournelle,

who was very much influenced by Piper and in many ways considers himself Beam's spiritual descendant—and incidently was John W. Campbell's last major *discovery*—has said that sometimes, when he's gotten down a particularly good line, he can hear the "old man" chuckle and whisper, *atta boy*.

Introduction

Dr. John D. Clark

THE SILICONE WORLD

1. THE STAR AND ITS MOST IMPORTANT PLANET

The planet is named Uller (it seems that when interstellar travel was developed, the names of Greek Gods had been used up, so those of Norse gods were used). It is the second planet of the star Beta Hydri, right angle 0:23, declension -77:32, G-0 (solar) type star, of approximately the same size as Sol; distance from Earth, 21 light years.

Uller revolves around it in a nearly circular orbit, at a distance of 100,000,000 miles, making it a little colder than Earth. A year is of the approximate length of that on Earth. A day lasts 26 hours.

The axis of Uller is in the same plane as the orbit, so that at a certain time of the year the north pole is pointed directly at the sun, while at the opposite end of the orbit it points directly away. The result is highly exaggerated seasons. At the poles the temperature runs from 120°C to a low of -80°C. At the equator it remains not far from 10°C all year round. Strong winds blow during the summer and winter, from the hot to the cold pole; few winds during the spring and fall.

The appearance of the poles varies during the year from baked deserts to glaciers covered with solid CO_2. Free water exists in the equatorial regions all year round.

2. SOLAR MOVEMENT AS SEEN FROM ULLER

As seen from the north pole—no sun is visible on Jan. 1. On April 1, it bisects the horizon all day, swinging completely around. April 1 to July 1, it continues swinging around, gradually rising in the sky, the spiral converging to its center at the zenith, which it reaches July 1. From July 1 to October 1 the spiral starts again, spreading out from the center until on October 1 it bisects the horizon again. On October 1 night arrives to stay until April 1.

At the equator, the sun is visible bisecting the southern horizon for all 26 hours of the day on January 1. From January 1 to April 1, the sun starts to dip below the horizon at night, to rise higher above it during the day. During all this time it rises and sets at the same hours, but rises in the southeast and sets in the southwest. At noon it is higher each day in the southern sky until April 1, when it rises due east, passes through the zenith and sets due west. From April 1 to July 1, its noon position drops down to the north, until on July 1, it is visible all day, bisected by the northern horizon.

3. CHEMISTRY AND GEOLOGY OF ULLER

Calcium and chlorine are rarer than on earth, sodium is somewhat commoner. As a result of the shortage of calcium there is a higher ration of silicates to carbonates than exists on earth. The water is slightly alkaline and resembles a very dilute solution of sodium silicate (water glass). It would have a pH of 8.5 and tastes slightly soapy. Also, when it dries out it leaves a sticky, and then a glassy, crackly film. Rocks look fairly earthlike, but the absence or scarcity of anything like limestone is noticeable. Practically all the sedimentary rocks are of the sandstone type.

All rivers are seasonal, running from the polar regions to the central seas in the spring only, or until the polar cap is completely dried out.

4. ANIMAL LIFE

As on Earth life arose in the primitive waters and with a carbon base, but because of the abundance of silicone, there was a strong tendency for the microscopic organisms to develop silicate exoskeletons, like diatoms. The present invertebrate animal life of the planet is of this type and is confined to the equatorial seas. They run from amoeba-like objects to things like crayfish, with silicate skeletons. Later, some species of them started taking silicone into their soft tissues, and eventually their carbon-chain compounds were converted to silicone type chains, from

$$\begin{array}{ccc} | & | & | \\ -\,C\,-\,C\,-\,C\,- \\ | & | & | \end{array} \quad \text{to} \quad \begin{array}{ccc} | & | & | \\ O\,-\,Si\,-\,O\,-\,Si\,-\,O\,-\,Si, \\ | & | & | \end{array}$$

with organic radicals on the side links. These organisms were a transitional type, with silicone tissues and water body fluids, resembling the earthly amphibians, and are now practically extinct. There are a few species, something like segmented worms, still to be seen in the backwaters of the central seas.

A further development occurred when the silicone chain animals began to get short-chain silicones into their circulatory systems, held in solution by OH or NH_2 groups on the ends and branches of the chains. The proportion of these compounds gradually increased until the water was a minor and then a missing constituent. The larger mobile species were, then, practically anhydrous. Their blood consists of short-chain silicones, with quartz reinforcing for the soft parts and their armor, teeth, etc., of pure amorphous quartz (opal). Most of these parts are of the milky variety, variously tinted with metallic impurities, as are the varieties of sapphires.

These pure silicone animals, due to their practical indestructibility, annihilated all but the smaller of the carbon animals, and drove the compromise types into odd corners as relics. They developed into a fish-like animal with a very large swim-bladder to compensate for the rather higher density of the silicone tissues, and from these fish the land animals developed. Due to their high density and resulting high weight, they tend to be low on the ground, rather reptilian in look. Three pairs of legs are usual in order to distribute the heavy load. There is no sharp dividing line between the quartz armor and the silicone tissue. One merges into the other.

The dominant pure silicone animals only could become mobile and venture far from the temperate equatorial regions of Uller, since they neither froze nor stiffened with cold, nor became incapacitated by heat. Note that all animal life is cold-blooded, with a negligible difference between body and ambient temperatures. Since the animals are silicones, they don't get sluggish like cold snakes.

5. PLANT LIFE

The plants are of the carbon-metabolism, silicate-shell type, like the primitive animals. They spread out from the equator as far as they could go before the baking polar summers killed them. They have normal seasonal growth in the temperate zones and remain dormant and frozen in the winter. At the poles there is no vegetation, not because of the cold winter, but because of the hot summer. The winter winds frequently blow over dead trees and roll them as far as the equatorial seas. Other dead vegetation, because of the highly silicious water, always gets petrified unless it is eaten first. What with the quartz-speckled hides of the living vegetation and the solid quartz of the dead, a forest is spectacular.

The silicone animals live on the plants. They chew them up, dehydrate them, and convert their silicious outer bark and carbonaceous interiors into silicones for themselves. When silicone tissue is metabolized, the carbon and hydrogen go to CO_2 and H_2O, which are breathed out, while the silicone goes into SiO_2, which is deposited as more teeth and armor. (Compare the terrestrial octopus, which makes armor-plating out of calcium urate instead of excreting urea or uric acid.) The animals can, of course, eat each other too, or make a meal of the small carbonaceous animals of the equatorial seas.

Further note that the animals cannot digest plants when they are cold. They can eat them and store them, but the disposal of the solid water and CO_2 is too difficult a problem. When they warm up, the water in the plants melts and can be disposed of, and things are simpler.

II
THE FLUORINE PLANET

1. THE STAR AND PLANET

The planet named Niflheim is the fourth planet of Nu Puppis, right angle 6:36, declension -43:09; B8 type star, blue-white and hot, 148 light years distant from Earth, which will require a speed in excess of light to reach it.

Niflheim is 462,000,000 miles from its primary, a little less than the distance of Jupiter from our sun. It thus does not receive too great a total amount of energy, but what it does receive is of high potential, a large fraction of it being in the ultra-violet and higher frequencies. (Watch out for really super-special sunburn, etc., on unwarned personnel.)

The gravity of Niflheim is approximately 1 g, the atmospheric pressure approximately 1 atmosphere, and the average ambient temperature about -60°C; -76°F.

2. ATMOSPHERE

The oxidizer in the atmosphere is free fluorine (F_2) in a rather low concentration, about 4 or 5 percent. With it appears a mad collection of gases. There are a few inert diluents, such as N_2 (nitrogen), argon, helium, neon, etc., but the major fraction consists of CF_4 (carbon tetrafluoride), BF_3 (boron trifluoride), SiF_4 (silicon tetrafluoride), PF_5 (phosphorous pentafluoride), SF_6 (sulphur hexafluoride) and probably others. In other words, the fluorides of all the non-metals that can form fluorides. The phosphorous pentafluoride rains out when the weather gets cold. There is also free oxygen, but no chlorine. That would be liquid except in very hot weather. It sometimes appears combined with fluorine in chlorine trifluoride. The atmosphere has a slight yellowish tinge.

3. SOIL AND GEOLOGY

Above the metallic core of the planet, the lithosphere consists exclusively of fluorides of the metals. There are no oxides, sulfides, silicates or chlorides. There are small deposits of such things as bromine trifluoride, but these have no great importance. Since fluorides are weak mechanically, the terrain is flattish. Nothing tough like granite to build mountains out of. Since the fluoride ion is colorless, the color of the soil depends upon the predominant metal in the region. As most of the light metals also have colorless ions, the colored rocks are rather rare.

4. THE WATERS UNDER THE EARTH

They consist of liquid hydrofluoric acid (HF). It melts at -83°C and boils at 19.4°C. In it are dissolved varying quantities of metallic and non-metallic fluorides, such as boron trifluoride, sodium fluoride, etc. When the oceans and lakes freeze, they do so from the bottom up, so there is no layer of ice over free liquid.

5. PLANTS AND PLANT METABOLISM

The plants function by photosynthesis, taking HF as water from the soil, and carbon tetrafluoride as the equivalent of carbon dioxide from the air to produce chain compounds, such as:

$$
\begin{array}{ccccc}
& H & H & H & H \\
& | & | & | & | \\
-\!\!\! & C & -\!\! C & -\!\! C & -\!\! C & -\!\!\! \\
& | & | & | & | \\
& F & F & F & F
\end{array}
$$

and at the same time liberating free fluorine. This reaction could only take place on a planet receiving lots of ultra-violet because so much energy is needed to break up carbon tetrafluoride and hydrofluoric acid. The plant catalyst (doubling for the magnesium in chlorophyll) is nickel. The plants are colored in various ways. They get their metals from the soil.

6. ANIMALS AND ANIMAL METABOLISM

Animals depend upon two main reactions for their energy, and for the construction of their harder tissues. The soft tissues are about the same as the plant molecules, but the hard tissues are produced by the reaction:

$$
\begin{array}{ccc}
H & H & H \\
| & | & | \\
-C-C-C- \\
| & | & | \\
F & F & F
\end{array}
+ F_2 \rightarrow
\begin{array}{ccc}
F & F & F \\
| & | & | \\
-C-C-C- \\
| & | & | \\
F & F & F
\end{array}
+ HF
$$

resulting in a teflon boned and shelled organism. He's going to be tough to do much with. Diatoms leave strata of powdered teflon. The main energy reaction is:

$$
\begin{array}{ccc}
\text{H} & \text{H} & \text{H} \\
| & | & | \\
-\text{C}-\text{C}-\text{C}- & \cdots & +\ F_2 \rightarrow CF_4 + HF \\
| & | & | \\
\text{F} & \text{F} & \text{F}
\end{array}
$$

The blood catalyst metal is titanium, which results in colorless arterial blood and violet veinous, as the titanium flips back and forth between tri- and tetravalent states.

7. EFFECT ON INTRUDING ITEMS

Water decomposes into oxygen and hydrofluoric acid. All organic matter (earth type) converts into oxygen, carbon tetrafluoride, hydrofluoric acid, etc., with more or less speed. A rubber gas mask lasts about an hour. Glass first frosts and then disappears. Plastics act like rubber, only a little slower. The heavy metals, iron, nickel, copper, monel, etc., stand up well, forming an insoluble coat of fluorides at first and then doing nothing else.

8. WHY GO THERE?

Large natural crystals of fluorides, such as calcium difluoride, titanium tetrafluoride, zirconium tetrafluoride, are extremely useful in optical instruments of various forms. Uranium appears as uranium hexafluoride, all ready for the diffusion process. Compounds of such non-metals as boron are obtainable from the atmosphere in high purity with very little trouble. All metallurgy must be electrical. There are considerable deposits of beryllium, and they occur in high concentration in its ores.

PROLOGUE

On Satan's Footstool

The big armor-tender vibrated, gently and not unpleasantly, as the contragravity field alternated on and off, occasionally varying its normal rate of five hundred to the second when some thermal updraft lifted the vehicle and the automatic radar-altimeter control acted to alter the frequency and lower it again. Sometimes it rocked slightly, like a boat on the water, and, in the big screen which served in lieu of a window at the front of the control cabin, the dingy-yellow landscape would seem to tilt a little. If unshielded human eyes could have endured the rays of Nu Pupis, Niflheim's primary, the whole scene would have appeared a vivid Saint Patrick's Day green, the effect of the blue-predominant light on the yellow atmosphere. The outside 'visor-pickup, however, was fitted with filters which blocked out the gamma-rays and X-rays and most of the ultraviolet-rays, and added the longer light-waves of red and orange which were absent, so that things looked much as they would have under the light of a GO-type star like Sol. The air was faintly yellow, the sky was yellow with a greenish cast, and the clouds were green-gray.

A thousand feet below, the local equivalent of a forest grew, the trees, topped with huge ragged leaves, looking like hundred-foot stalks of celery. There would be animal life down there, too—little round things, four inches across, like eight-legged crabs, gnawing at the vegetation, and bigger things, two feet long, with articulated shell-armor and sixteen legs, which fed on the smaller herbivores. Beyond, in the middleground, was open grassland, if one could so call a mat of wormlike colorless or pastel-tinted sprouts, and a river meandered through it. On the skyline, fifty miles away, was a range of low dunes and hills, none more than a thousand feet high.

No human had ever set foot on the surface, or breathed the air, of Niflheim. To have done so would have been instant death; the air was a mixture of free fluorine and fluoride gasses, the soil was metallic fluorides, damp with acid rains, and the river was pure hydrofluoric acid. Even the ordinary spacesuit would have been no protection; the glass and rubber and plastic would have disintegrated in a matter of minutes. People came to Niflheim, and worked the mines and uranium refineries and chemical plants, but they did so inside power-driven and contragravity-lifted armor, and they lived on artificial satellites two thousand miles off-planet. This vehicle, for instance, was built and protected as no spaceship ever had to be, completely insulated and entered only through a triple airlock—an outer lock, which would be evacuated outward after it was closed, a middle lock kept evacuated at all times, and an inner lock, evacuated into the interior of the vehicle before the middle lock could be opened. Niflheim was worse than airless, much worse.

The chief engineer sat at his controls, making the minor lateral adjustments in the vehicle's position which were not possible to the automatic controls. One of the radiomen was receiving from the orbital base; the other was saying, over and over, in an exasperatedly patient voice: "Dr. Murillo. Dr. Murillo. Please come in, Dr. Murillo." At his own panel of instruments, a small man with grizzled black hair around a bald crown, and a grizzled beard, chewed nervously at the stump of a dead cigar and listened intently to what was—or for what wasn't—coming in to his headset receiver. A couple of assistants checked dials and refreshed their memories from note-books and peered anxiously into the big screen. A large, plump-faced, young man in soiled khaki shirt and shorts, with extremely hairy legs, was doodling on his notepad and eating candy out of a bag. And a black-haired girl in a suit of coveralls three sizes too big for her, and, apparently, not much of anything else, lounged with one knee hooked over her chair-arm, staring into the screen at the distant horizon.

"Dr. Murillo. Dr. Mur—" The radioman broke off in mid-syllable and listened for a moment. "I hear you, doctor, go ahead." Then, a moment later: "What's your position, now, doctor?"

"I can see them," the girl said, lifting a hand in front of her. "At two o'clock, about one of my hand's-breadths above the horizon."

The man with the grizzled beard put his face into the fur around the eyepiece of the telescopic-'visor and twisted a dial. "You have good eyes, Miss Quinton," he complimented. "Only four personal armors; Ahmed, ask him where the fifth is."

"We only see four of your personal-armors," the radioman said. "Who's missing, and why?" He waited for a moment, then lowered the hand-phone and turned. "The fifth one's inside the handling-machine. One of the Ullerans. Gorkrink."

The larger of the specks that had appeared on the horizon resolved itself into a handling-machine, a thing like an oversized contragravity-tank, with a bulldozer-blade, a stubby derrick-boom instead of a gun, and jointed, claw-tipped arms to the sides. The smaller dots grew into personal armor—egg-shaped things that sprouted arms and grab-hooks and pushers in all directions. The man with the grizzled beard began talking rapidly into his hand-phone, then hung it up. There was a series of bumps, and the armor-tender, weightless on contragravity, shook as the handling-machine came aboard.

"You ever see any nuclear bombing, Miss Quinton?" the young man with the hairy legs asked, offering her his candy bag.

"Only by telecast, back Sol-side," she replied, helping herself. "Test-shots at the Federation Navy proving-ground on Mars. I never even heard of nuclear bombs being used for mining till I came here, though."

"Well, if this turns out as well as the other job, three months ago, it'll be something to see," he promised. "These volcanoes have been dormant for, oh, maybe as long as a thousand years; there ought to be a pretty good head of gas down there. And the magma'll be thick, viscous stuff, like basalt on Terra. Of course, this won't be anything like basalt in composition—it'll be intensely compressed metallic fluorides, with a very high metal-content. The volcanoes we shot three months ago yielded a fine flow of lava with all sorts of metals—nickel, beryllium, vanadium, chromium, iridium, as well as copper and iron."

"What sort of gas were you speaking about?" she asked.

"Hydrogen. That's what's going to make the fireworks; it combines explosively with fluorine. The hydrogen-fluorine combination is what passes for combustion here; the result is hydrofluoric acid, the local equivalent of water. See, the metallic core of this planet is covered, much less thickly than that of Terra, with fluoride rock—fluorspar, and that sort of thing. There's nothing like granite here, for instance. That's why those big dunes, out there, are the best Niflheim has in the way of mountains. The subsurface hydrogen is produced when the acid filters down through the rock, combines with pure metals underneath."

"Dr. Murillo's inside, now," the radioman said. "Just came out of the inner airlock. He'll be up as soon as he gets out of his pressure-suit."

"As soon as he gets here, I'll touch it off," the bearded man said. "Everything set, de Jong?"

"Everything ready, Dr. Gomes," one of his assistants assured him.

The door at the rear of the control-cabin opened, and Juan Murillo, the seismologist, entered, followed by an assistant. Murillo was a big man, copper-skinned, barrel-chested; he looked like a third- or fourth-generation Martian, of Andes Indian ancestry. He came forward and stood behind Gomes' chair, looking down at the instruments. His assistant stopped at the door. This assistant was not human. He was a biped, vaguely humanoid, but he had four arms and a face like a lizard's, and, except for some equipment on a belt, he was entirely naked.

He spoke rapidly to Murillo, in a squeaking jabber. Murillo turned.

"Yes, if you wish, Gorkrink," he said, in the English-Spanish-Afrikaans-Portuguese mixture that was Sixth Century, A.E., Lingua Terra. Then he turned back to Gomes as the Ulleran sat down in a chair by the door.

"Well, she's all yours, Lourenço, shoot the works."

Gomes stabbed the radio-detonator button in front of him. A voice came out of the PA-speaker overhead: "In sixty seconds, the bombs will be detonated... thirty seconds...fifteen seconds...ten seconds... five seconds, four seconds, three seconds, two seconds, one second..."

Out on the rolling skyline, fifty miles away, a lancelike ray of blue-white light shot up into the gathering dusk—a clump of five rays, really, from five deep shafts in an irregular pentagon half a mile across, blended into one by the distance. An instant later, there was a blinding flash, like sheet-lightning, and a huge ball of varicolored fire belched upward, leaving a series of smoke-rings to float more slowly after it. That fireball flattened, then spread to form the mushroom-head of a column of incandescent gas that mounted to overtake it, engorging the smoke-rings as it rose, twisting, writhing, changing shape, turning to dark smoke in one moment and belching flame and crackling with lightning the next. The armor-tender began to pitch and roll; it was all the engineer and one of the assistants could do, together, to keep it level.

"In about half an hour," the large young man told the girl, "the real fireworks should be starting. What's coming up now is just small debris from the nuclear blast. When the shockwaves get down far enough to crack things open, the gas'll come up, and then steam and ash, and then the magma. This one ought to be twice as good as the one we shot three months ago; it ought to be every bit as good as Krakatoa, on Terra, in 59 Pre-Atomic."

"Well, even this much was worth staying over for," the girl said, watching the screen.

"You going on to Uller on the *City of Canberra?*"

Lourenço Gomes asked. "I wish I were; I have to stay over and make another shot, in a month or so, and I've had about all of Niflheim I can take, now. The sooner I get onto a planet where they don't ration the air, the better I'll like it."

"Well, what do you know!" the large young man with the hairy legs mock-marveled. "He doesn't like our nice planet!"

"Nice planet!" Gomes muttered something. "They call Terra God's Footstool; well, I'll give you one guess who uses this thing to prop his cloven hoofs on."

"When are you going to Terra?" the girl asked him.

"Terra? I don't know, a year, two years. But I'm going to Uller on the next ship—the *City of Pretoria*—if we get the next blast off in time. They want me to design some improvements on a couple of power-reactors, so I'll probably see you when I get there."

"Here she comes!" the chief engineer called. "Watch the base of the column!"

The pillar of fiery smoke and dust, still boiling up from where the bombs had gone off far underground, was being violently agitated at the bottom. A series of new flashes broke out, lifting and spreading the incandescent radioactive gasses, and then a great gush of flame rose. A column of pure hydrogen must have rushed up into the vacuum created by the explosion; the next blast of flame, in a lateral sheet, came at nearly ten thousand feet above the ground, and great rags of fire, changing from red to violet and back through the spectrum to red again, went soaring away to dissipate in the upper atmosphere. Then geysers of hot ash and molten rock spouted upward; some of the white-hot debris landed almost at the acid river, half-way to the armor-tender.

"We've started a first-class earthquake, too," the Hispano-Indian Martian Murillo said, looking at the instruments. "About six big cracks opening in the rock-structure. You know, when this quiets down and cools off, we'll have more ore on the surface than we can handle in ten years, and more than we could have mined by ordinary means in fifty."

About four miles from the original blast, another eruption began with a terrific gas-explosion.

"Well, that finishes our work," the large young man said, going to a kitbag in the corner of the cabin and getting out a bottle. "Get some of those plastic cups, over there, somebody; this one calls for a drink."

"That's right," Gomes said. "You do something once, it may be an accident; you repeat the performance, and it's a success." He began pushing papers aside on his desk, and the girl in the too-ample coveralls brought drinking cups.

The Ulleran, in the background, rose quickly and squeaked apologetically. Murillo nodded. "Yes, of course, Gorkrink. No need for you to stay here." The Ulleran went out, closing the door behind him.

"That taboo against Ullerans and Terrans watching each other eat and drink," Murillo said. "What is that, part of their religion?"

"No, it's their version of modesty," the girl replied. "Like some of our sex-inhibitions, which they can't even begin to understand...But you were speaking to him in Lingua Terra; I didn't know any of them understood it."

"Gorkrink does," Murillo said, uncorking the bottle and pouring into the plastic cups. "None of them can speak it, of course, because of the structure of their vocal organs, any more than we can speak their languages without artificial aids. But I can talk to him

in Lingua Terra without having to put one of those
damn gags in my mouth, and he can pass my instruc-
tions on to the others. He's been a big help; I'll be
sorry to lose him."

"Lose him?"

"Yes, his year's up; he's going back to Uller on
the *Canberra*. You know, it's impossible to keep some
trace of fluorine from the air in the handling-machines,
or even out on the orbiters, and it plays the devil with
their lungs. He wanted to stay on another three months,
to help with the next shot, but the medics wouldn't
hear of it. . . . He's from Keegark, wherever on Uller
that is; claims to be a prince, or something. I know
all the other geeks kowtow to him. But he's a damn
good worker. Very smart; picks things up the first
time you tell him. I'll recommend him unqualifiedly
for any kind of work with contragravity or mechanized
equipment."

They all had drinks, now, except the chief engineer, who wanted a rain-check on his.

"Weil, here's to us," Murillo said. "The first A-
bomb miners in history . . ."

I -

Commander-in-Chief
Front and Center

General Carlos von Schlichten threw his cigarette away, flexed his hands in his gloves, and set his monocle more firmly in his eye, stepping forward as the footsteps on the stairway behind him ceased and the other officers emerged from the squat flint keep—Captain Cazabielle, the post CO; big, chocolate-brown Brigadier-General Themistocles M'zangwe; little Colonel Hideyoshi O'Leary. Far in front of him, to the left, the horizon was lost in the cloudbank over Takkad Sea; directly in front, and to the right, the brown and gray and black flint mountains sawed into the sky until they vanished in the distance. Unseen below, the old caravan-trail climbed one side of the pass and slid down the other, a sheer five hundred feet below the parapet and the two corner catapult-platforms which now mounted 90-mm guns. On the little hundred-foot-square parade ground in front of the keep, his aircar was parked, and the soldiers were assembled.

Ten or twelve of them were Terrans—a couple of lieutenants, sergeants, gunners, technicians, the sergeant-driver and corporal-gunner of his own car. The other fifty-odd were Ulleran natives. They stood erect on stumpy legs and broad, six-toed feet. They had four arms apiece, one pair from true shoulders and the other connected to a pseudo-pelvis midway down the torso. Their skins were slate-gray and rubbery, speckled with pinhead-sized bits of quartz that had been formed from perspiration, for their body-tissues were silicone instead of carbon-hydrogen. Their narrow heads were unpleasantly saurian; they had small, double-lidded red eyes, and slit-like nostrils, and wide mouths filled with opalescent teeth. Except for their belts and equipment, they were completely naked; the uniform consisted of the emblem of the Chartered Uller Company stencil-painted on chests and backs. Clothing, to them, was unnecessary, either for warmth or modesty. As to the former, they were cold-blooded and could stand a temperature-range of from a hundred and twenty to minus one hundred Centigrade. Von Schlichten had seen them sleeping in the open with their bodies covered with frost or freezing rain; he had also seen them wade through boiling water. As to the second, they had practically no sex-inhibitions; they were all of the same gender, true, functional, hermaphrodites. Any individual among them could bear young, or fertilize the ova of any other individual. Fifteen years ago, when he had come to Uller as a former Terran Federation captain newly commissioned colonel in the army of the Uller Company, it had taken some time before he had become accustomed to the detailing of a non-com and a couple of privates out of each platoon for baby-sitting duty. At least, though, they didn't have the squaw-trouble around army posts on Uller that they had on Thor, where he had last been stationed.

An airjeep, coming in out of the sun, circled the crag-top fort and let down onto the terrace next to von Schlichten's command-car. It carried a bristle of 15-mm machine-guns, and two of the eight 50-mm rocket-tubes on either side were empty and freshly smoke-stained. The duraglass canopy slid back, and the two-man crew—lieutenant-driver and sergeant-gunner— jumped out. Von Schlichten knew them both.

"Lieutenant Kendall; Sergeant Garcia," he greeted. "Good afternoon, gentlemen."

Both saluted, in the informal, hell-with-rank-we're- all-human manner of Terran soldiers on extraterres- trial duty, and returned the greeting.

"How's the Jeel situation?" he asked, then nodded toward the fired rocket-tubes. "I see you had some shooting."

"Yes, sir," the lieutenant said. "Two bands of them. We sighted the first coming up the eastern side of the mountain about two miles this side of the Blue Springs. We got about half of them with MG-fire, and the rest dived into a big rock-crevice. We had to use two rockets on them, and then had to let down and pot a few of them with our pistols. We caught the second band in that little punchbowl place about a mile this side of Zortolk's Old Fort. There were only six of them; they were bunched together, feeding. Off one of their own gang, I'd say; the way we've been keep- ing them up in the high rocks, they've been eating inside the family quite a bit, lately. We let them have two rockets. No survivors. Not many very big pieces, in fact. We let down at Zortolk's for a beer, after that, and Captain Martinelli told us that one of his jeeps caught what he thinks was the same band that was down off the mountain night-before-last and ate those peasants on Prince Neeldink's estate."

"By God, I'm glad to hear that!" There'd been a perfect hell of a flap about that business. Before the Terrans came to Uller, it was a good year when not more than five hundred farm-folk would be killed and eaten by Jeel cannibals. The incident of two nights ago had been the first of its kind in almost six months, but the nobleman whose serfs had been eaten was practically accusing the Company of responsibility for the crime. "I'll see that Neeldink is informed. The more you do for these damned geeks, the more they expect from you. . . . When you get your vehicle re-ammoed, lieutenant, suppose you buzz back to where you machine-gunned that first gang. If there are any more around, they'll have moved in for the free meal by now." This breakdown of the Jeels' taboo against eating fellow-tribesmen was one of the best things he'd heard from the cannibal-extermination project for some time.

He turned to Themistocles M'zangwe. "In about two weeks, get a little task-force together. Say ten combat-cars, about twenty airjeeps, and a battalion of Kragan Rifles in troop-carriers. Oh, yes, and this good-for-nothing Konkrook Fencibles outfit of Prince Jaiz-erd's; they can be used for beaters, and to block escape routes." He turned back to Lieutenant Kendall and Sergeant Garcia. "Good work, boys. And if the syn-chro-photos show that any of that first bunch got away, don't feel too badly about it. These Jeels can hide on the top of a pool-table."

He climbed into the command-car, followed by Themistocles M'zangwe and Hideyoshi O'Leary. Ser-geant Harry Quong and Corporal Hassan Bogdanoff took their places on the front seat; the car lifted, turned to nose into the wind, and rose in a slow spiral. Below, the fort grew smaller, a flat-topped rectangle of ma-sonry overlooking the pass, a gun covering each ap-proach, and two more on the square keep to cover the rocky hogback on which the fort had been built, with the flagpole between them. Once that pole had lifted a banner of ragged black marsh-flopper skin bearing the device of the Kragan riever-chieftain whose family had built the castle; now it carried a neat rectangle of blue bunting emblazoned with the wreathed globe of the Terran Federation and, below that, the blue-gray pennant which bore the vermilion trademark of the Chartered Uller Company.

"Where now, sir?" Harry Quong asked.

He looked at his watch. Seventeen-hundred; there wasn't time for a visit to Zortolk's Old Fort, ten miles to the north at the next pass.

"Back to Konkrook, to the island."

The nose of the car swung east by south; the cold-jet rotors began humming and then the hot-jets were cut in. The car turned from the fort and the mountains and shot away over the foothills toward the coastal plain. Below were forests, yellow-green with new foliage of the second growing season of the equatorial year, veined with narrow dirt roads and spotted with occasional clearings. Farther east, the dirty gray woodsmoke of Uller marked the progress of the char-coal-burnings. It took forty years to burn the forests clear back to the flint cliffs; by the time the burners reached the mountains, the new trees at the seaward edge would be ready to cut. Off to the south, he could see the dark green squares, where the hemlocks and Norway spruce had been planted by the Company. With a little chemical fertilizer, they were doing well, and they made better charcoal than the silicate-heavy native wood. That was the only natural fuel on Uller; there was no coal, of course, since fallen timber and even standing dead trees petrified in a matter of a couple of years. There was too much silica on Uller, and not enough of anything else; what would be coal-seams on Terra were strata of silicified wood. And, of course, there was no petroleum. There was less charcoal being burned now than formerly; the Uller

Company had been bringing in great quantities of
synthetic thermoconcentrate-fuel, and had been setting up nuclear furnaces and nuclear-electric power-
plants, wherever they gained a foothold on the planet.

Beyond the forests came the farmlands. Around
the older estates, thick walls of flint and petrified
wood had been built, and wide moats dug, to keep
out the shellosaurs. But now the moats were dry, and
the walls falling into disrepair. Some of the newer
farms, land devoted to agriculture with the declining
demand for charcoal, had neither moats nor walls.
That was the Company, too; the huge shell-armored
beasts had become virtually extinct in the Konk Isthmus now, since the introduction of bazookas and recoilless rifles. There seemed to be quite a bit of power-
equipment working in the fields, and big contragravity
lorries were drifting back and forth, scattering fertilizer, mainly nitrates from Mimir or Yggdrasill. There
were still a good number of animal-drawn plows and
harrows in use, however.

As planets went, Uller was no bargain, he thought
sourly. At times, he wished he had never followed
the lure of rapid promotion and fantastically high pay
and left the Federation regulars for the army of the
Uller Company. If he hadn't, he'd probably be a colonel, at five thousand sols a year, but maybe it would
be better to be a middle-aged colonel on a decent
planet—Odin, with its two moons, Hugin and Munin,
and its wide grasslands and its evergreen forests that
looked and even smelled like the pinewoods of Terra,
or Baldur, with snow-capped mountains, and clear,
cold lakes, and rocky rivers dashing under great vine-
hung trees, or Freya, where the people were human
to the last degree and the women were so breathtak-
ingly beautiful—than a Company army general at

twenty-five thousand on this combination icebox, furnace, wind-tunnel and stonepile, where the water tasted
like soapsuds and left a crackly film when it dried;
where the temperature ranged, from pole to pole, between two hundred and fifty and minus a hundred and
fifty Fahrenheit and the Beaufort-scale ran up to thirty;
where nothing that ran or swam or grew was fit for
a human to eat, and where the people. . . .

Of course, there were worse planets than Uller.
There was Nidhog, cold and foggy, its equatorial zone
a gloomy marsh and the rest of the planet locked in
eternal ice. There was Bifrost, which always kept the
same face turned to its primary; one side blazingly
hot and the other close to absolute zero, with a narrow
and barely habitable twilight zone between. There was
Mimir, swarming with a race of semi-intelligent quasi-
rodents, murderous, treacherous, utterly vicious. Or
Niflheim. The Uller Company had the franchise for
Niflheim, too; they'd had to take that and agree to
exploit the planet's resources in order to get the franchise for Uller, which furnished a good quick measure
of the comparative merits of the two.

Ahead, the city of Konkrook sprawled along the
delta of the Konk river and extended itself inland. The
river was dry, now. Except in spring, when it was a
red-brown torrent, it never ran more than a trickle,
and not at all this late in the northern summer. The
aircar lost altitude, and the hot-jet stopped firing. They
came gliding in over the suburbs and the yellow-green
parks, over the low one-story dwellings and shops,
the lofty temples and palaces, the fantastically twisted
towers, following a street that became increasingly
mean and squalid as it neared the industrial district
along the waterfront.

Von Schlichten, on the right, glanced idly down,

puffing slowly on his cigarette. Then he stiffened, the muscles around his right eye clamping tighter on the monocle. Leaning forward, he punched Harry Quong lightly on the shoulder.

"Circle back, sergeant; let's have a look at that street again," he directed. "Something going on, down there; looks like a riot."

"Yes, sir; I saw it," the Chinese-Australian driver replied. "Terrans in trouble; bein' mobbed by geeks. Aircar parked right in the bloody middle of it."

The car made a twisting, banking loop and came back, more slowly. Colonel Hideyoshi O'Leary was using the binoculars.

"That's right," he said. "Terrans being mobbed. Two of them, backed up against a house. I saw one of them firing a pistol."

Von Schlichten had the handset of the car's radio, and was punching out the combination of the Company guardhouse on Gongonk Island; he held down the signal button until he got an answer.

"Von Schlichten, in car over Konkrook. Riot on Fourth Avenue, just off Seventy-second Street." No Terran could possibly remember the names of Konkrook's streets; even native troops recruited from outside found the numbers easier to learn and remember. "Geeks mobbing a couple of Terrans. I'm going down, now, to do what I can to help; send troops in a hurry. Kragan Rifles. And stand by; my driver'll give it to you as it happens."

The voice of somebody at the guardhouse, bawling orders, came out of the receiver as he tossed the phone forward over Harry Quong's shoulder; Quong caught it and began speaking rapidly and urgently into it while he steered with the other hand. Von Schlichten took one of the five-pound spiked riot-maces out of the rack in front of him. Themistocles M'zangwe had already drawn his pistol; he shifted it to his left hand and took a mace in his right. The Nipponese-Irish colonel, looking like a homicidally infuriated pixie, had an automatic in one hand and a long dagger in the other.

Harry Quong and Hassan Bogdanoff were old Uller hands; they'd done this sort of work before. Bogdanoff rose into the ball-turret and swung the twin 15-mm's around, cutting loose. Quong brought the car in fast, at about shoulder-height on the mob. Between them, they left a swath of mangled, killed, wounded, and stunned natives. Then, spinning the car around, Quong set it down hard on a clump of rioters as close as possible to the struggling group around the two Terrans. Von Schlichten threw back the canopy and jumped out of the car, O'Leary and M'zangwe behind him.

There was another aircar, a dark maroon civilian job, at the curb; its native driver was slumped forward over the controls, a short crossbow-bolt sticking out of his neck. Backed against the closed door of a house, a Terran with white hair and a small beard was clubbing futilely with an empty pistol. He was wounded, and blood was streaming over his face. His companion, a young woman in a long fur coat, was laying about her with a native bolo-knife.

Von Schlichten's mace had a spiked ball-head, and a four-inch spike in front of that. He smashed the ball down on the back of one Ulleran's head, and jabbed another in the rump with the spike.

"Zak! Zak!" he yelled, in pidgin-Ulleran. "Jik-jik, you lizard-faced Creator's blunder!"

The Ulleran whirled, swinging a blade somewhere between a big butcherknife and a small machete. His mouth was open, and there was froth on his lips.

"Znidd suddabit!" he screamed.

Von Schlichten parried the cut on the steel shaft of his mace. *"Suddabit* yourself, you geek bastard!" he shouted back, ramming the spike-end into the opal-filled mouth. "And *znidd* you, too," he added, recovering and slamming the ball-head down on the narrow saurian skull. The Ulleran went down, spurting a yellow fluid about the consistency of gun-oil. Then, without wasting words, he maced another of the things.

Ahead, one of the natives had caught the wounded Terran with both lower hands, and was raising a dagger with his upper right. The girl in the fur coat swung wildly, slashing the knife-arm, then chopped down on the creature's neck. To one side, a native somewhat better dressed than the others, to the extent of a couple of belts with gold ornaments, drew a Terran automatic. Von Schlichten hurled his mace and drew his pistol, thumbing off the safety as he swung it up, but before he could fire, Hassan Bogdanoff had seen and swung his guns around; the double burst caught the native in the chest and fairly tore him apart.

Another of them closed with the girl, grabbing her right arm with all four hands and biting at her; she screamed and kicked her attacker in the groin, where an Ulleran is, if anything, even more vulnerable than a Terran. The native howled hideously, and von Schlichten, jumping over a couple of corpses, shoved the muzzle of his pistol into the creature's open mouth and pulled the trigger, blowing its head apart like a rotten pumpkin and splashing both himself and the girl with yellow blood and rancid-looking gray-green brains.

Hideyoshi O'Leary, jumping forward after von

Schlichten, stuck his dagger into the neck of a rioter
and left it there, then caught the girl around the waist
with his free arm. Themistocles M'zangwe dropped
his mace and swung the frail-looking man onto his
back. Together, they struggled back to the command-
car, von Schlichten covering the retreat with his pistol.
Another rioter—a Zirk nomad from the North, he
guessed—was aiming one of the long-barreled native
air-rifles, holding the ten-inch globe of the air-cham-
ber in both lower hands. Von Schlichten shot him,
and the Zirk literally blew to pieces.

For an instant, he wondered how the small burst-
ing-charge of a 10-mm explosive pistol-bullet could
accomplish such havoc, and assumed that the native
had been carrying a bomb in his belt..Then another
explosion tossed fragmentary corpses nearby, and another and another. Glancing quickly over his shoulder,
he saw four combat-cars coming in, firing with 40-
mm auto-cannon and 15-mm machine-guns. They
swept between the hovels on one side and the ware-
houses on the other, strafing the mob, darted up to a
thousand feet, looped, and came swooping back, and
this time there were three long blue-gray troop-carriers
behind them.

These landed in the hastily cleared street and began
disgorging native Company soldiers—Kragan mercenaries, he noted with satisfaction. They carried a
modified version of the regular Terran Federation infantry rifle, stocked and sighted to conform to their
physical peculiarities, with long, thorn-like, triangular
bayonets. One platoon ran forward, dropped to one
knee, and began firing rapidly into what was left of
the mob. Four-handed soldiers can deliver a simply
astonishing volume of fire, particularly when armed
with auto-rifles having twenty-shot drop-out maga-

zines which can be changed with the lower hands
without lowering the weapon.

There was a clatter of shod hoofs, and a company
of the King of Konkrook's cavalry came trotting up
on their six-legged, lizard-headed, quartz-speckled
mounts. Some of these charged into side alleys, joy-
fully lancing and cutting down fleeing rioters, while
others dismounted, three tossing their reins to a fourth,
and went to work with their crossbows. Von Schlichten, who ordinarily entertained a dim opinion of the
King of Konkrook's soldiery, admitted, grudgingly,
that it was smart work; four hands were a big help in
using a crossbow, too.

A Terran captain of native infantry came over,
saluting.

"Are you and your people all right, general?" he
asked.

Von Schlichten glanced at the front seat of his car,
where Harry Quong, a pistol in his right hand, was
still talking into the radio-phone, and Hassan Bogdanoff was putting fresh belts into his guns. Then he
saw that the Graeco-African brigadier and the Irish-
Japanese colonel had gotten the wounded man into
the car. The girl, having dropped her bolo, was leaning against the side of the car, one foot heedlessly in
what was left of an Ulleran who had gotten smashed
under it, weak with nervous reaction.

"We seem to be, Captain Pedolsky. Very smart
work; you must have those vehicles of yours on hy-
perspace-drive. . . . How is he, colonel?"

"We'd better get him to the hospital, right away,"
O'Leary replied. "I think he has a concussion."

"Harry, call the hospital. Tell them what the score
is, and tell them we're bringing the casualty in to their
top landing stage . . . Why, we'll make out very nicely,

captain. You'd better stay around with your Kragans and make sure that these geeks of King Jaikark's don't let the riot flare up again and get away from them. And don't let them get the impression that they can maintain order around here without our help; the Company would like to see that attitude discouraged."

"Yes, sir, I understand." Captain Pedolsky opened the pouch on his belt and took out the false palate and tongue-clicker without which no Terran could do more than mouth a crude and barely comprehensible pidgin-Ulleran. Stuffing the gadget into his mouth, he turned and began jabbering orders.

Von Schlichten helped the girl into the car, placing her on his right. The wounded civilian was propped up in the left corner of the seat, and Colonel O'Leary and Brigadier-General M'zangwe took the jump-seats. The driver put on the contragravity-field, and the car lifted up.

"Them, see if there's a flask and a drinking-cup in the door pocket next to you," he said. "I think Miss Quinton could use a drink."

The girl turned. Even in her present disheveled condition, she was beautiful—a trifle on the petite side, with black hair and black eyes that quirked up oddly at the outer corners. Her nails were black-lacquered and spotted with little gold stars, evidently a new feminine fad from Terra.

"I certainly could, general. . . . How did you know my name?"

"You've been on Uller for the last three months; ever since the *City of Canberra* got in from Niflheim. On Uller, there aren't enough of us that everybody doesn't know all about everybody else. You're Dr. Paula Quinton; you're an extraterrestrial sociographer, and you're a field-agent for the Extraterrestrials' Rights

Association, like Mohammed Ferriera, here." He took the cup and flask from Themistocles M'zangwe and poured her a drink. "Take this easy, now; Baldur honey-rum, a hundred and fifty proof."

He watched her sip the stuff cautiously, cough over the first mouthful, and then get the rest of it down.

"More?" When she shook her head, he stoppered the flask and relieved her of the cup. "What were you doing in that district, anyhow?" he wanted to know. "I'd have thought Mohammed Ferriera would have had more sense than to take you there, or go there, himself, for that matter."

"We went to visit a friend of his, a native named Keeluk, who seems to be a sort of combination clergyman and labor leader," she replied. "I'm going to observe labor conditions at the North Pole mines in a short while, and Mr. Keeluk was going to give me letters of introduction to friends of his at Skilk."

With the aid of his monocle, von Schlichten managed to keep a straight face. Neither M'zangwe nor O'Leary had any such aid; the African rolled his eyes and the Japanese-Irishman grimaced.

"We talked with Mr. Keeluk for a while," the girl said, "and when we came out, we found that our driver had been killed and a mob had gathered. Of course, we were carrying pistols; they're part of this survival-kit you make everybody carry, along with the emergency-rations and the water-desilicator. Mr. Ferriera's wasn't loaded, but mine was. When they rushed us, I shot a couple of them, and then picked up that big knife...."

"That's why you're still alive," von Schlichten commented.

"We wouldn't be if you hadn't come along," she told him. "I never in my life saw anything as beautiful

as you coming through that mob swinging that war-
club!"

"Well, I never saw anything much more beautiful
than those 40-mm's beginning to land in the mob,"
von Schlichten replied.

The aircar swung out over Konkrook Channel and
headed toward the blue-gray Company buildings on
Gongonk Island, and the Company airport, swarming
with lorries and airboats, where the ten thousand-ton
Oom Paul Kruger had just come in from Keegark,
and the Company's one real warship, the cruiser *Procyon,* was lifting out for Grank, in the North. Down
at the southern tip of the island, the three-thousand-
foot globe of the spaceship *City of Pretoria,* from
Niflheim, was loading with cargo for Terra.

"Just what happened, while you and Mr. Ferriera
were in Keeluk's house. Miss Quinton?" Hideyoshi
O'Leary asked, trying not to sound official. "Was
Keeluk with you all the time? Or did he go out for a
while, say fifteen or twenty minutes before you left?"

"Why, yes, he did." Paula Quinton looked surprised. "How did you guess it? You see, a dog started
barking, behind the house, and he excused himself
and . . ."

"A dog?" von Schlicten almost shouted. The other
officers echoed him, and on the front seat, Harry
Quong said, "Coo-bli'me!"

"Why, yes . . ." Paula Quinton's eyes widened. "But
there are no dogs on Uller, except a few owned by
Terrans. And wasn't there something about . . . ?"

Von Schlichten had the radio-phone and was calling the command car at the scene of the riot. The
sergeant-driver answered.

"Von Schlichten here; my compliments to Captain
Pedolsky, and tell him he's to make immediate and

thorough search of the house in front of which the incident occurred, and adjoining houses. For his information, that's Keeluk's house. Tell him to look for traces of Governor-General Harrington's collie, or any of the other terrestrial animals that have been disappearing—that goat, for instance, or those rabbits. And I want Keeluk brought in, alive and in condition to be interrogated. I'll send more troops, or Constabulary, to help you." He handed the phone to M'zangwe. "You take care of that end of it, Them; you know who can be spared."

"But, what . . . ?" the girl began.

"That's why you were attacked," he told her. "Keeluk was afraid to let you get away from there alive to report hearing that dog, so he went out and had a gang of thugs rounded up to kill you."

"But he was only gone five minutes."

"In five minutes, I can put all the troops in Konkrook into action. Keeluk doesn't have radio or TV— we hope—but he has his forces concentrated, and he has a pretty good staff."

"But Mr. Keeluk's a friend of ours. He knows what our Association is trying to do for his people . . ."

"So he shows his appreciation by setting that mob on you. Look, he has a lot of influence in that section. When you were attacked, why wasn't he out trying to quiet the mob?"

"When they jumped you, you tried to get back into the house," M'zangwe put in. "And you found the door barred against you."

"Yes, but . . ." The girl looked troubled; M'zangwe had guessed right. "But what's all the excitement about the dog? What is it, the sacred totem-animal of the Uller Company?"

"It's just a big brown collie, named Stalin, like

half the dogs on Terra. Somebody stole it, and Keeluk was keeping it, and we want to know why. We don't like geek mysteries; not when they lead to murderous attacks on Terrans, at least."

The aircar let down on the hospital landing stage. A stretcher was waiting, with a Terran interne and two Ulleran orderlies. They got the still-unconscious Mohammed Ferriera out of the car.

"You'd better go with them, yourself, Miss Quinton," von Schlichten advised. "You have a couple of nasty-looking bruises and bumps. A couple of abrasions, too, where those geeks grabbed you; they have hides like sandpaper. And better have that coat cleaned, before that goo on it hardens, or it'll be ruined."

"Yes. You have a lot of it on your uniform, too."

He glanced down at the blue-gray jacket. "So I have. And another thing. Those letters Keeluk was going to give you, the ones to his friends in Skilk. Did you get them?"

She felt in the pocket of her coat. "Yes. I still have them."

"I wish you'd let Colonel O'Leary have a look at them. There may be more to them than you think... Hid, will you go with Miss Quinton?"

II-

Rakkeed, Stalin, and the Rev. Keeluk

Von Schlichten, in a fresh uniform, sat at the end of the table in Sidney Harrington's office; Harrington and Eric Blount, the Lieutenant-Governor, faced each other across it, over the three-foot disc of an Ulleran chess-board. Harrington had the white, or center, position. Blount, sandy-haired and considerably younger, was playing black, and his pieces were closing in relentlessly from the outer rim.

"Well, then what?" Harrington asked.

Von Schlichten dropped ash from his cigarette into the tray that served all three of them.

"Nothing much," he replied. "Keeluk bugged out as soon as he saw my car let down. We picked up a few of his ragtag-and-bobtail, and they're being questioned now, but I doubt if they'll tell us anything we don't know already. The dog had been kept in a lean-to back of the house; it had been removed, probably as soon as Keeluk called in his goon-gang. At least one of the rabbits had been kept on the premises, too, some time ago. No trace of the goat."

He watched Blount move one of his pieces and nodded approvingly. "The riot's been put down," he continued, "but we're keeping two companies of Kragans in the city, and about a dozen airjeeps patrolling the section from Eightieth down to Sixty-fourth, and from the waterfront back to Eighth Avenue. There is also the equivalent of a regiment of King Jaikark's infantry—spearmen, crossbowmen, and a few riflemen—and two of those outsize cavalry companies of his, helping hold the lid down. They're making mass arrests, indiscriminately. More slaves for Jaikark's court favorite, of course."

"Or else Gurgurk wants them to use for patronage," Blount added. "He's been building quite a political organization, lately. Getting ready to shove Jaikark off the throne, I'd say."

Harrington pushed one of his pieces out along a radial line toward the rim. Blount promptly took a pawn, which, under Ulleran rules, entitled him to a second move. He shifted another piece, a sort of combination knight and bishop, to threaten the piece Harrington had moved.

"Oh, Gurgurk wouldn't dare try anything like that," the Governor-General said. "He knows we wouldn't let him get away with it. We have too much of an investment in King Jaikark."

"Then why's Gurgurk been supporting this damned Rakkeed?" Blount wanted to know, hastily interposing a piece. "Gurgurk can follow one of two lines of policy. He can undertake to heave Jaikark off the throne and seize power, or he has to support Jaikark on the throne. We're subsidizing Jaikark. Rakkeed has been preaching this crusade against the Terrans, and against Jaikark, whom we control. Gurgurk has been subsidizing Rakkeed..."

"You haven't any proof of that," Harrington protested.

"My Intelligence Section has," von Schlichten put in. "We can give sums of money, and dates, and the names of the intermediaries through whom they were paid to Rakkeed. Eric is absolutely correct in making that statement."

"Personally, I think Gurgurk's plan is something like this: Rakkeed will stir up anti-Terran sentiment here in Konkrook, and direct it against our puppet, Jaikark, as well as against us," Blount said. "When the outbreak comes, Jaikark will be killed, and then Gurgurk will step in, seize the Palace, and use the Royal army to put down the revolt that he's incited in the first place. That will put him in the position of the friend of the Company, and most of his dupes will be rounded up and sold as slaves, and King Gurgurk'll pocket the proceeds. The only question is, will Rakkeed let himself be used that way? I think Rakkeed's bigger than Gurgurk ever can be. And more of a threat to the Company. Everywhere we turn, Rakkeed's at the bottom of whatever happens to be wrong. This business, for instance; Keeluk's one of Rakkeed's followers."

"Eric, you have Rakkeed on the brain!" Harrington exclaimed impatiently, then moved the threatened piece counterclockwise on the circle where he had placed it. "He's just a barbarian caravan-driver."

Eric Blount moved the piece that had taken Harrington's pawn.

"Your king's in danger," he warned. "And Hitler was just a paper-hanger."

"Rakkeed has no following, except among the rabble." Harrington puffed furiously at his pipe, trying to figure the best protection for his king.

"You just think he hasn't," Blount retorted. "Here in Konkrook, he's always entertained by one or another of the big ship-owning nobles. They probably deprecate his table-manners, but they just love his politics. And the same thing at Keegark, and at the Free Cities along the Eastern Shore."

"The last time Rakkeed was in Konkrook, he was the guest of the Keegarkan Ambassador," von Schlichten stated. "Intelligence got that from a spy we'd planted among the embassy servants."

"You sure this spy wasn't just romancing?" Harrington asked. "You get so confounded many wild stories about Rakkeed. Three days after he was reported here at Konkrook, he was reported at Skilk, five thousand miles away, said to be having an audience with King Firkked."

"No mystery to that," von Schlichten said. "He travels on our ships, in disguise, coolie-class, on the geek-deck."

"Be a good idea if he could be caught at it, some time," Blount said, making another move. "One of the lower-deck loading ports could be left unlocked, by carelessness, and he could blunder overboard at about five thousand feet." He watched Harrington make a deceptively pointless-looking move. "Sid, this damn dog business worries me."

"Worries me, too. I'm fond of that mutt, and God only knows what sort of stuff he's been getting to eat. And I hate to think of why those geeks stole him, too."

"Well, at risk of seeming heartless, I'm not so much worried for Stalin as I am about why Keeluk was hiding him, and why he was willing to murder the only two Terrans in Konkrook who trust him, to prevent our finding out that he had him."

"A Mr. Keeluk, a clergyman," von Schlichten quoted. He chain-lit another cigarette and stubbed out the old one. "Maybe the Rev. Keeluk wanted Stalin for sacramental purposes."

Blount looked up sharply. "Ritual killing?" he asked. "Or sympathetic magic?"

Von Schlichten shrugged. "Take your choice. Maybe Rakkeed wanted the dog, to kill before a congregation of his followers, killing us by proxy, or in effigy. Or maybe they think we worship Stalin, and getting control of him would give them power over us. I wish we knew a little more about Ulleran psychology."

That wasn't the first time he'd made that wish. Even if sex weren't the paramount psychological factor the ancient Freudians believed, it was an extremely important one, and on Uller most of the fundamental terms of Terran psychology were meaningless. At the same time, the average Ulleran probably had complexes and neuroses that would have had Freud talking to himself, and they certainly indulged in practices that would have even stood Krafft-Ebing's hair on end.

"One thing," Blount said. "It doesn't take any Ulleran psychologist to know that about eighty percent of them hate us poisonously."

"Oh, rubbish!" Harrington blew the exclamation out around his pipe-stem with a gush of smoke. "A few fanatics hate us, and a few merchants who lost money when we replaced this primitive barter economy of theirs, but nine-tenths of them have benefitted enormously from us, and continue to benefit. . . ."

"And hate us more deeply with each new benefit," Blount added. "They resent everything we've done for them."

"Yes, this spaceport proposition of King Orgzild of Keegark looks like it, now doesn't it?" Harrington retorted. "He hates and resents us so much that he's offered us a spaceport at his city. . . ."

"What's it going to cost him?" Blount asked. "He furnishes the land—sequestered from the estate of some noble he executed for treason—and the labor— all forced. We furnish the structural steel, the machine-equipment, the engineering. We get a spaceport we don't really need, and he gets all the business it'll bring to Keegark. Considering the fact that Rakkeed is a welcome guest at his embassy here, and at the Royal Palace at Keegark, I'm beginning to wonder if he isn't fomenting trouble for us here at Konkrook to make us willing to move our main base to his city."

He made a move. Instantly, Harrington slashed out from the middle of the board with one of his heavy-duty, all-purpose pieces and took a piece, then moved again.

"Now look whose king's threatened!" he crowed.

"Yes, I see." Blount brought a piece clockwise around the board and took the threatening piece, then moved again. "I hope you see whose king's threatened, now."

Harrington swore, reached out to move a piece, and then jerked his hand back as though the piece were radioactive. For a while, he sat puffing his pipe and staring at the board.

"In fact, Orgzild's so sure that we're going to accept his offer that he's started building two new power-reactors, to handle the additional power-demand that'll result from the increased business," Blount continued.

"Where's he getting the plutonium?" von Schlichten asked.

"Where can he get it?" Harrington replied. "He just bought four tons of it from us, off the *City of Pretoria*."

"That's a hell of a lot of plutonium," Blount said. "I wonder if he mightn't have some idea of what else plutonium can be used for, beside generating power."

"Oh, God, I hope not!" Harrington exclaimed. "You're going to get me started seeing burglars under the bed, next. . . ."

"Maybe there are burglars," Blount said, pointing with his cigarette-holder to Harrington's threatened king. "Can't you do something about that, Sid?" Then he turned to von Schlichten. "Before we get off the subject, how about those letters the Rev. Keeluk gave to the Quinton girl?"

"All addressed to Skilkans known to be Rakkeed disciples and rabidly anti-Terran," von Schlichten replied. "We radioed the list to Skilk; Colonel Cheng-Li, our intelligence man there, teleprinted us back a lot of material on them that looks like the Newgate Calendar. We turned the letters themselves over to Doc Petrie, the Ulleran philology sharp, who is a pretty fair cryptanalyst. He couldn't find any indications of cipher, but there was a lot of gossip about Keeluk's friends and parishioners which might have arbitrary code-meanings. I'm going to explain the situation to Miss Quinton, and advise her to have nothing to do with any of the people Keeluk gave her letters to."

Harrington had gotten his king temporarily out of danger, losing a piece doing it.

"Think she'll listen to you?" he asked. "These Extraterrestrials' Rights Association people are a lot of blasted fanatics, themselves. We're a gang of bloody-handed, flint-hearted, imperialistic sons of bitches in their book, and anything we say's sure to be a Hitler-sized lie."

"Oh, they're not as bad as all that. I never met the girl before today, but old Mohammed Ferriera's a decent bloke. And their association's really done a lot of good. For one thing, they put an end to the peonage system on Yggdrasill, and I know what conditions were like, there, before they did."

A calculating look came into Harrington's eye. He puffed slowly at his pipe and slid a piece from the center toward the sector of the board nearest him. Blount whistled softly and made a quick re-arrangement.

"Carlos, did you say she told you she was going to Skilk, in the near future?" Harrington asked. "Well, look here; you're going up that way, yourself, with that battalion of Kragans, on the *Aldebaran*. Why don't you invite her to make the trip with you? You can be quite attractive to young ladies, when you try, and she'll be grateful for that rescue this afternoon, which is always a good foundation. Maybe you can plant a couple of ideas where they'll do the most good. She's only been here for three months—since the *Canberra* got in from Niflheim. You know and I know and we all know that there are a lot of things up there at the polar mines that would look like hell to anybody who didn't understand local conditions. . . ."

"Well, Miss Quinton's company won't be any particularly heavy cross for me to bear," von Schlichten replied. "I won't guarantee anything, of course. . . ."

The intercom-speaker on the table whistled several times. Harrington swore, laid down his pipe, and got up, brushing ashes from the front of his coat. He flipped a switch and spoke into the box.

"Governor," a voice replied out of it, "there's a geek procession just landed from a water-barge in front, and is coming up the roadway to Company House. A platoon of Jaikark's Household Guards, with rifles; the Spear of State; a royal litter; about thirty geek nobles, on foot; a gift-litter; another pla-

toon of riflemen, if you say the last syllable quick
enough."

"That'll be Gurgurk, coming to tell us how un-
happy his Sodden and Inebriated Geekship is about
that fracas on Seventy-second Street," Harrington said.
"The gift-litter will contain the customary indemnity,
at the current market quotation. Have Gurgurk and
party admitted, all but the rifle-platoons; give him an
honor guard of our Kragans, and keep his own gun-
toters outside. Take them to the Reception Hall, and
hold them there till I signal from the Audience Hall,
and then herd them in."

He came back and made a move. Immediately,
Blount took one of his pieces, moved again, took
another, and made the third move to which he was
entitled.

"I'll mate you in four moves," he predicted. "Want
to play it out, before we go down?"

"Sure; what's time to a geek? Gurgurk'd think we
were worried about something if we didn't keep him
waiting. . . . Good Lord! You do have me over a bar-
rel, Eric!"

III -

Four-and-Twenty
Geek Heads

Governor-General Sidney Harrington sat on the comfortably upholstered bench on the dais of the Audience Hall, flanked by von Schlichten and Eric Blount. He didn't look particularly regal, even on that high seat— with his ruddy outdoorsman's face and his ragged gray mustache and his old tweed coat spotted with pipe-ashes, he might have been any of the dozen-odd country-gentleman neighbors of von Schlichten's boyhood in the Argentine. But then, to a Terran, any of the kings of Uller would have looked like a freak birth in a lizard-house at a zoo; it was hard to guess what impression Harrington would make on an Ulleran.

He took the false palate and tongue-clicker, officially designated as an "enunciator, Ulleran" and, colloquially, as a geek-speaker, out of his coat pocket and shoved it into his mouth. Von Schlichten and Blount put in theirs, and Harrington pressed the floor-button with his toe. After a brief interval, the wide doors at the other end of the hall slid open, and the Konkrookan notables, attended by a dozen Company native-officers and a guard of Kragan Rifles, entered. The honor-guard advanced in two columns; between them marched an unclad and heavily armed native carrying an ornate spear with a three-foot blade upright in front of him with all four hands. It was the Konkrookan Spear of State; it represented the proxy-pres-

36

ence of King Jaikark. Behind it stalked Gurgurk, the
Konkrookan equivalent of Prime Minister or Grand
Vizier; he wore a gold helmet and a thing like a string-
vest made of gold wire, and carried a long sword with
a two-hand grip, a pair of Terran automatics built for
a hand with six four-knuckled fingers, and a pair of
matched daggers. He was considerably past the Ulleran prime of life—seventy or eighty, to judge from
the worn appearance of his opal teeth, the color of
his skin, and the predorrinantly reddish tint of his
quartz-speckles. An immature Ulleran would be a very
light gray, white under the arms, and his quartz-specks
would run from white to pale yellow. The retinue of
nobles behind Gurgurk ran through the whole spectrum, from a princeling who was almost oyster-gray
to old Ghroghrank, the Keegarkan Ambassador, who
was even blacker and more red-speckled than Gurgurk. All of them carried about as much ironmongery
as the Prime Minister—the pistols were all Terran,
and the swords and daggers were mostly made either
on Terra or at the Terran-operated steel-works on Vol-
und.

Four slaves brought up in the rear carrying an or-
nately inlaid box on poles. When the spear-bearer
reached the exact middle of the hall, he halted and
grounded his regalia-weapon with a thump. Gurgurk
came up and halted a couple of paces behind and to
the left of the spear, and all the other nobles drew up
in two curved lines some ten paces to the rear, with
considerable pushing and jostling and a *sotto voce*
argument, with overtones of weapon-fingering, about
precedence. All, that is, but Ghroghrank and another
noble, who came up and planted themselves beside
Gurgurk. Von Schlichten regarded the assemblage

sourly through his monocle. Maybe Sid Harrington
did look regal, after all.

The Governor-General rose slowly and descended
from the dais, advancing to within ten paces of the
Spear, von Schlichten and Blount accompanying him.
Out of the corner of his eye, von Schlichten watched
a couple of Kragan mercenaries with fifty-shot ma-
chine-rifles move unobtrusively to positions from
whence they could, if necessary, spray the visitors
with bullets without endangering the Terrans.

"Welcome, Gurgurk," Harrington gibbered through
his false palate. "The Company is honored by this
visit."

"I come in the name of my royal master, His Sublime and Ineffable Majesty, Jaikark the Seventeenth,
King of Konkrook and of all the lands of the Konk
Isthmus," Gurgurk squeaked and clicked. "I have the
honor to bring with me the Lord Ghroghrank, Ambassador of King Orgzild of Keegark to the court of
my royal master."

"And I," Ghorghrank said, after being suitably wel-
comed, "am honored to be accompanied by Prince
Gorkrink, special envoy from my master, his Royal
and Imperial Majesty King Orgzild, who is in your
city to receive the shipment of power-metal my royal
master has been honored to be permitted to purchase
from the Company."

More protocol about welcoming Gorkrink. Then
Gurgurk cleared his throat with a series of barking
sounds.

"My royal master, His Sublime and Ineffable Majesty, is prostrated with grief," he stated solemnly.
"Were his sorrow not so overwhelming, he would
have come in His Own Sacred Person to express the
pain and shame which he feels that people of the

Company should be set upon and endangered in the streets of the royal city."

If he weren't doped to the ears, von Schlichten substituted mentally. There was a native drug which had, on its users, the combined effects of hashish, heroin and yohimbine; Jaikark and all his court circle were addicts. He probably hadn't even heard of the riot.

"The soldiers of His Sublime and Ineffable Majesty came most promptly to the aid of the troops of the Company, did they not, General von Schlichten?" Harrington asked.

"Within minutes, Your Excellency," von Schlichten replied gravely. "Their promptness, valor, and efficiency were most exemplary."

Gurgurk spoke at length, expressing himself as delighted, on behalf of his royal master, at hearing such high praise from so distinguished a soldier. Eric Blount then contributed a short speech, beseeching the gods that the deep and beautiful friendship existing between the Chartered Uller Company and His Sublime etcetera would continue unimpaired, and that His Sublime etcetera would enjoy long life and peaceful reign, managing, by a trick of Konkrookan grammar, to imply that the second would be conditional upon the first. The Keegarkan Ambassador then spoke his piece, expressing on behalf of King Orgzild the deepest regret that the people of the Company should be so molested, and managing to hint that things like that simply didn't happen at Keegark.

The Prince Gorkrink then spoke briefly, in sympathy for the great and good friend of all Ulleran peoples, Mohammed Ferriera, who had been injured, and hoping that he would soon enjoy full health again. He also managed to convey King Orgzild's pleasure at having obtained the plutonium. Von Schlichten noticed that a few of his more recent quartz-specks were slightly greenish in tinge, a sure sign that he had, not long ago, been exposed to the fluorine-tainted air which men and geeks alike breathed on Niflheim. When a geek prince hired out as a laborer for a year on Niflheim, he did so for only one purpose—to learn Terran technologies.

Gurgurk then announced that so enormous a crime against the friends of His Sublime etcetera had not been allowed to go unpunished, signaling behind him with one of his lower hands for the box to be brought forward. The slaves carried it to the front, set it down, and opened it, taking from it a rug which they spread on the floor. On this, from the box, they placed twenty-four newly severed opal-grinning heads, in four neat rows. They had all been freshly scrubbed and polished, but they still smelled like crushed cockroaches.

The three Terrans looked at them gravely. A double-dozen heads was standard payment for an attack in which no Terran had been killed. Ostensibly, they were the heads of the ringleaders: in practice, they were usually lopped from the first two-dozen prisoners or over-age slaves at hand, without regard for whether the victims had even heard of the crime which they were expiating. If the Extraterrestrial's Rights Association were really serious about the rights of these geeks, they'd advocate booting out all these native princes and turning the whole planet over to the Company. That had been the Terran Federation's idea, from the beginning; why else give the Company's chief representative the title of Governor-General?

There was another long speech from Gurgurk, with the nobles behind him murmuring antiphonal agree-

ment—standard procedure, for which there was a
standard pun, geek chorus—and a speech of response
from Sid Harrington. Standing stiffly through the whole
rigamarole, von Schlichten waited for it to end, as
finally it did.

They walked back from the door, whence they had
escorted the delegation, and stood looking down at
the saurian heads on the rug. Harrington raised his
voice and called to a Kragan sergeant whose chevrons
were painted on all four arms.

"Take this carrion out and stuff it in the incinera-
tor," he ordered. "If any of you think you can clean
up this rug and this box, you're welcome to them."

"Wait a moment," von Schlichten told the sergeant.
Then he disgorged and pouched his geek-speaker. "See
that head, there?" he asked, rolling it over with his
toe. "I killed that geek, myself, with my pistol, while
Them and Hid were getting Ferriera into the car. Miss
Quinton killed that one with the bolo; see where she
chopped him on the back of the neck? The cut that
took off the head was a little low, and missed it. And
Hid O'Leary stuck a knife in that one." He walked
around the rug, turning heads over with his foot. "This
was cut-rate head-payment; they just slashed off two-
dozen heads at the scene of the riot. I don't like this
butchery of worn-out slaves and petty thieves any
better than anybody else, but this I don't like either.
Six months ago, Gurgurk wouldn't have tried to pull
anything like this. Now he's laughing up his non-
existent sleeve at us."

"That's what I've been preaching, all along," Eric
Blount took up after him. "These geeks need having
the fear of Terra thrown into them."

"Oh, nonsense, Eric; you're just as bad as Carlos,

here!" Harrington tut-tutted. "Next, you'll be saying that we ought to depose Jaikark and take control ourselves."

"Well, what's wrong with that, for an idea?" von Schlichten demanded. "Don't you think we could? Our Kragans could go through that army of Jaikark's like fast neutrons through toilet-paper."

"My God!" Harrington exploded. "Don't let me hear that kind of talk again! We're not *conquistadores;* we're employees of a business concern, here to make money honestly, by exchanging goods and services with these people...."

He turned and walked away, out of the Audience Hall, leaving von Schlichten and Blount to watch the removal of the geek-heads.

"You know, I went a little too far," von Schlichten confessed. "Or too fast, rather. He's got to be conditioned to accept that idea."

"We can't go too slowly, either," Blount replied. "If we wait for him to change his mind, it'll be the same as waiting for him to retire. And that'll be waiting too long."

Von Schlichten nodded seriously. "Did you notice the green specks in the hide of that Prince Gorkrink?" he asked. "He's just come back from Niflheim. Not on the *Pretoria,* I don't think. Probably on the *Canberra,* three months ago."

"And he's here to get that plutonium, and ship it to Keegark on the *Oom Paul Kruger,*" Blount considered. "I wonder just what he learned, on Niflheim."

"I wonder just what's going on at Keegark," von Schlichten said. "Orgzild's pulled down a regular First-Century-model iron curtain. You know, four of our best native Intelligence operatives have been murdered in Keegark in the last three months, and six more have just vanished there."

"Well, I'm going there in a few days, myself, to talk to Orgzild about this spaceport deal," Blount said. "I'll have a talk with Hendrik Lemoyne and Mac-Kinnon. And I'll see what I can find out for myself."

"Well, let's go have a drink," von Schlichten suggested, consulting his watch. "About time for a cocktail."

IV-

If You Read It
in Stanley-Browne

Von Schlichten and Blount entered the bar together—
the Broadway Room, decorated in gleaming plastics
and chromium in enthusiastic if slightly inaccurate
imitation of a First Century New York nightclub. There
were no native servants to spoil the illusion, such as
it was: the service was fully automatic. Going to a
bartending machine, von Schlichten dialed the cocktail they had decided upon and inserted his key to
charge the drinks to his account, filling a four-portion
jug.

As they turned away, they almost collided with
Hideyoshi O'Leary and Paula Quinton. The girl wore
a long-sleeved gown to conceal a bandage on her right
wrist, and her face was rather heavily powdered in
spots; otherwise she looked none the worse for recent
experiences.

"Well, you seem to have gotten yourself repaired,
Miss Quinton," he greeted her. "Feel better,
now?...Miss Quinton, this is Lieutenant-Governor
Blount. Eric, Miss Paula Quinton."

"Delighted, Miss Quinton," Blount said. "Carlos
tells us he found you standing over poor Mohammed
Ferriera, fighting like a commando. How is Mohammed, by the way? No danger, I hope; we all like
him."

Mohammed Ferriera was still unconscious, the girl

reported; he had a minor concussion, but the medics were not greatly disturbed, and expected him to be fully recovered in a few weeks. Von Schlichten invited her and her escort to join him and Blount. Colonel O'Leary was carrying a cocktail jug and a couple of glasses; finding a table out of the worst of the noise, they all sat down together.

"I suppose you think it's a joke, our being nearly murdered by the people we came to help," Paula began, a trifle defensively.

"Not a very funny joke," von Schlichten told her. "It's been played on us till it's lost its humor."

"Yes, geek ingratitude's an old story to all of us," Blount agreed. "You stay on this planet very long and you'll see what I mean."

"You call them that, too?" she asked, as though disappointed in him. "Maybe if you stopped calling them geeks, they wouldn't resent you the way they do. You know, that's a nasty name; in the First Century Pre-Atomic, it designated a degraded person who performed some sort of revolting public exhibition. . . ."

"Biting off live chickens' heads, in a sideshow wild-man act," Hideyoshi O'Leary supplied. "When you get up north, watch how the peasants kill these little things like six-legged iguanas that they raise for food."

"That isn't the reason, though," von Schlichten said. "As we use it, the word's pure onomatopoeia. You've learned some of the languages; you know what they sound like. *Geek-geek-geek.*"

"As far as that goes, you know what the geek name for a Terran is?" Blount asked. *"Suddabit."*

She looked puzzled for a moment, then slipped in her enunciator. Even in the absence of any native, she used her handkerchief to mask the act.

"Suddabit," she said, distinctly. "Sud-da-a-bit." Taking out the geek-speaker, she put it away. "Why, that's exactly how they'd pronounce it!"

"And don't tell me you haven't heard it before," O'Leary said. "The geeks were screaming it at you, over on Seventy-second Street, this afternoon. *Znidd suddabit;* kill the Terrans. That's Rakkeed the Prophet's whole gospel."

"So you see," Eric Blount rammed home the moral, "this is just another case of nobody with any right to call anybody else's kettle black. . . . Cigarette?"

"Thank you." She leaned toward the lighter-flame O'Leary had snapped into being. "I suspect that of being a principle you'd like me to bear in mind at the polar mines, when I see, let's say, some laborer being beaten by a couple of overseers with three foot lengths of three-quarter-inch steel cable."

"Well, you could also remember that a native's skin is about half an inch thick, and a good deal tougher than a human's," von Schlichten told her. "And it wouldn't hurt any if you found out how these laborers are treated at home. Mostly they're serfs hired from the big landowners; it's a fact you can easily verify that permission to join the labor-companies at the polar mines is regarded as a privilege, granted as a reward or denied as a punishment. And most of the geek landowners are bitterly critical of the way we treat our labor at the mines; they claim we make them dissatisfied with the treatment they get at home."

"Of course, they're always glad to have the peasants taken off their hands during a slack agricultural season," Blount added, "and we train workers to handle contragravity power-equipment. I won't deny that there's a lot of unnecessary brutality on the part of the native foremen and overseers, which we're trying, gradually, to eliminate. You'll have to remember, though, that we're dealing with a naturally brutal race."

"Of course, mistreatment of native labor is always blamed on other natives, never on the gentle and kindly Terrans," she replied. "That's been SOP on every planet our Association's had any experience with."

"Now look; you just came here from Niflheim," von Schlichten objected. "The Company employs quite a few geeks there; how much brutality did you run into there?"

"Well, I must admit, the Ullerans who work there are very well treated. Except that I don't think it's right to employ any people with silicone body-tissues where they're going to breathe fluorine-tainted air."

"Nobody ought to be employed on that planet!" Hideyoshi O'Leary declared. "I did a two-year hitch there, when I was first commissioned in the Company service."

"I put in two years there, too," Blount supported him. "And I might add that that's a year longer than any Ulleran native is ever allowed to spend on Niflheim. You know what the set-up is, there, don't you? The Terran Federation Space Navy discovered and explored both Uller and Niflheim, which made both planets public domain. The Company was originally formed to exploit Uller alone, but the Federation insisted that both planets would have to be franchised to the same company. They wanted Niflheim exploited, mainly because of the uranium-deposits there. As it turned out, the Company's making as much money out of Niflheim as we are out of Uller."

"What you miss is this," von Schlichten pointed

out. "On Niflheim, there are about a thousand Terrans, and not more than five hundred geeks, all employed on construction-work and in the mines, on the planet itself, working directly under Terran supervision. We use them because they have four hands, and in the power-driven contragravity armor that's necessary there, they can manipulate more controls and do more things at once than we can. Here on Uller, at the polar mines, there are about ten thousand geeks working under five hundred Terrans, and most of the latter are engineers or technicians who don't do supervisory work. So we have to use native foremen, and they're guilty of what mistreatment the workers suffer."

"And remember, too," O'Leary added, "work at the polar mines can only go on for about two months out of the year—mid-September to mid-November at the Arctic, and mid-March to mid-May at the Antarctic. Naturally, things have to be done in a hurry and under pressure."

"Well, why do you work mines at the poles? Aren't there mineral deposits in places where you can work all year 'round?"

"Not as rich, or as accessible," Blount said. "You know what the seasons are like, at the poles of this planet. The temperature will range from about two-fifty Fahrenheit in mid-summer to a hundred and fifty below in winter. There's the most intense sort of thermal erosion you can imagine—the ice-cap melts in the spring to a sea, which boils away completely by the middle of the summer. There will be violent circular storms of hot wind, blowing away the light sand and dust and leaving the heavier particles of metallic ores and metals behind. Then, when the winds fall, we move in for a couple of months. It isn't really mining, or even quarrying; we just scoop up ore from the surface, load it onto ore-boats, and fly it down to Skilk and Krink and Grank, where it's smelted through the winter. The natives run the smelters; use the heat to thaw frozen food for themselves and their livestock while they're melting the ore. In the north, metallurgy . and food-preparation have always been combined that way."

"Yes, if you think the natives who work at the mines feel themselves ill-treated, you might propose closing them down entirely and see what the native reaction would be," von Schlichten told her. "Independently hired free workers can make themselves rich, by native standards, in a couple of seasons; many of the serfs pick up enough money from us in incentive-pay to buy their freedom after one season."

"Well, if the Company's doing so much good on this planet, how is it that this native, Rakkeed, the one you call the Mad Prophet, is able to find such a following?" Paula demanded. "There must be something wrong somewhere."

"That's a fair question," Blount replied, inverting a cocktail jug over his glass to extract the last few drops. "When we came to Uller, we found a culture roughly like that of Europe during the Seventh Century Pre-Atomic, or, more closely, like that of Japan before the beginning of the First Century P. A. We initiated a technological and economic revolution here, and such revolutions have their casualties, too. A number of classes and groups got squeezed pretty badly, like the horse-breeders and harness-manufacturers on Terra by the invention of the automobile, or the coal and hydroelectric interests when direct conversion of nuclear energy to electric current was developed, or the railroads and steamship lines at the time of the discovery of the contragravity-field. Naturally, there's a lot of ill-feeling on the part of merchants and artisans who weren't able or willing to adapt themselves to changing conditions; they're all backing Rakkeed and yelling *'Znidd suddabit!'* now. You know, it's a shame that geek messiah isn't a smart crook, instead of an honest fanatic; he could take in the equivalent of a couple of million sols a year off the North Uller merchants and the Equatorial Zone shipowners. But it is a fact, which not even Rakkeed can successfully deny, that we've raised the general living standard of this planet by about two hundred percent."

"Rakkeed is a Zirk," von Schlichten said. "They're the nomads who hire out to the northern merchants as caravan-drivers, and also prey, or used to prey, on the caravans as brigands. Since our air-freighters got into operation, neither caravan-driving nor caravan-raiding has been a paying business, and our air-patrols have made caravan-raiding suicidal as well. So the Zirks don't like us. The only thing they know or are willing to learn is handling these six-legged riding- and pack-animals we call hipposaurs. We employ a few of them as cavalry, and a few more of them work as the local equivalent of *gauchos,* and the rest just sit around and listen to Rakkeed's sermons."

Both jugs were empty. Colonel O'Leary, as befitted his junior rank, picked them up; after a good-natured wrangle with von Schlichten, Blount handed the colonel his credit-key.

"The merchants in the north don't like us; beside spoiling the caravan-trade, we're spoiling their local business, because the land-owning barons, who used to deal with them, are now dealing directly with us.

At Skilk, King Firkked's afraid his feudal nobility is going to try to force a Runnymede on him, so he's been currying favor with the urban merchants; that makes him as pro-Rakkeed and as anti-Terran as they are. At Krink, King Jonkvank has the support of his barons, but he's afraid of his urban bourgeoisie, and we pay him a handsome subsidy, so he's pro-Terran and anti-Rakkeed. At Skilk, Rakkeed comes and goes openly; at Krink he has a price on his head."

"Jonkvank is not one of the assets we boast about too loudly," Hideyoshi O'Leary said, pausing on his way from the table. "He's as bloody-minded an old murderer as you'd care not to meet in a dark alley anywhere."

"We can turn our backs on him and not expect a knife between our shoulders, anyhow," von Schlichten said. "And we can believe, oh, up to eighty percent of what he tells us, and that's sixty percent better than any of the other native princes, except King Kankad, of course. The Kragans are the only real friends we have on this planet." He thought for a moment. "Miss Quinton, are you doing sociographic research-work here, in addition to your Ex-Rights work?" he asked. "Well, let me advise you to pay some attention to the Kragans. You'll only find them treated at any length at all in that compendium of misinformation, Willard Stanley-Browne's *Short Sociographic History of Beta Hydrae II*, and ninety percent of what Stanley-Browne says about them is completely erroneous."

"Oh, but they're just a parasite-race on the Terrans," Dr. Paula Quinton objected. "You find races like that all through the explored galaxy—pathetic cultural mongrels."

Both men laughed heartily. Colonel O'Leary, returning with the jugs, wanted to know what he'd missed. Blount told him.

"Ha! She's been reading that thing of Stanley-Browne's," he said.

"What's the matter with Stanley-Browne?" Paula demanded.

"Stanley-Browne is one author you can depend on," O'Leary assured her. "If you read it in Stanley-Browne, it's wrong. You know, I don't think she's run into many Kragans. We ought to take her over and introduce her to King Kankad."

Von Schlichten allowed himself to be smitten by an idea. "By Allah, so we had!" he exclaimed. "Look, you're going to Skilk, in the next week, aren't you? Well, do you think you could get all your end-jobs cleared up here and be ready to leave by 0800 Tuesday? That's four days from today."

"I'm sure I could. Why?"

"Well, I'm going to Skilk, myself, with the armed troopship *Aldebaran*. We're stopping at King Kankad's Town to pick up a battalion of Kragan Rifles for duty at the polar mines, where you're going. Suppose we leave here in my command-car, go to Kankad's Town, and wait there till the *Aldebaran* gets in. That would give us about two to three hours. If you think the Kragans are 'pathetic cultural mongrels,' what you'll see there will open your eyes. And I might add that the nearest Stanley-Browne ever came to seeing Kankad's Town was from the air, once, at a distance of four miles."

"Well, they live entirely by serving as mercenary soldiers for the Uller Company, don't they?"

"More or less. You see, when we came to Uller, they were barbarian brigands; had a string of forts along caravan-roads and at fords and mountain-passes, and levied tolls. They raided into Konkrook and Keegark territory, too. Well, we had to break that up. We fought a little war with them, beat them rather badly in a couple of skirmishes, and then made a deal with them. That was before my time, when old Jerry Kirke was Governor-General. He negotiated a treaty with their King, bought their rievers'-forts outright, and paid them a subsidy to compensate for loss of tolls and raid-spoil, and agreed to employ the whole tribe as soldiers. We've taught them a lot—you'll see how much when you visit their town—but they aren't cultural mongrels. You'll like them."

"Well, general, I'll take you up," she said. "But I warn you; if this is some scheme to indoctrinate me with the Uller Company's side of the case and blind me to unjust exploitation of the natives here, I don't propagandize very easily."

"Fair enough, as long as you don't let fear of being propagandized blind you to the good we're doing here, or impair your ability to observe and draw accurate conclusions. Just stay scientific about it and I'll be satisfied. Now, let's take time out for lubrication," he said, filling her glass and passing the jug.

Two hours and five cocktails later, they were still at the table, and they had taught Paula Quinton some twenty verses of *The Heathen Geeks, They Wear No Breeks,* including the four printable ones.

V-

You Can Depend on It
It's Wrong

Gongonk Island, with its blue-gray Company buildings, and the Terran green of the farms, and the spaceport with its ring of mooring-pylons empty since the *City of Pretoria* had lifted out, two days before, for Terra, was dropping away behind. Von Schlichten held his lighter for Paula Quinton, then lit his own cigarette.

"I was rather horrified, Friday afternoon, at the way you and Colonel O'Leary and Mr. Blount were blaspheming against Stanley-Browne," she said. "His book is practically the sociographers' Koran for this planet. But I've been checking up, since, and I find that everybody who's been here any length of time seems to deride it, and it's full of the most surprising misstatements. I'm either going to make myself famous or get burned at the stake by the Extraterrestrial Sociographic Society after I get back to Terra. In the last three months, I've been really too busy with Ex-Rights work to do much research, but I'm beginning to think there's a great deal in Stanley-Browne's book that will have to be reconsidered."

"How'd you get into this, Miss Quinton?" he asked.

"You mean sociography, or Ex-Rights? Well, my father and my grandfather were both extraterrestrial sociographers—anthropologists whose subjects aren't anthropomorphic—and I majored in sociography at the University of Montevideo. And I've always been in sympathy with extraterrestrial races; one of my great-grandmothers was a Freyan."

"The deuce; I'd never have guessed that, as small and dark as you are."

"Well, another of my great-grandmothers was Japanese," she replied. "The family name's French. I'm also part Spanish, part Russian, part Italian, part English . . . the usual modern Argentine mixture."

"I'm an Argentino, too. From La Rioja, over along the Sierra de Velasco. My family lived there for the past five centuries. They came to the Argentine in the Year Three, Atomic Era."

"On account of the Hitler bust-up?"

"Yes. I believe the first one, also a General von Schlichten, was what was then known as a war-criminal."

"That makes us partners in crime, then," she laughed. "The Quintons had to leave France about the same time; they were what was known as collaborationists."

"That's probably why the Southern Hemisphere managed to stay out of the Third and Fourth World Wars," he considered. "It was full of the descendants of people who'd gotten the short end of the Second."

"Do you speak the Kragan language, general?" she asked. "I understand it's entirely different from the other Equatorial Ulleran languages."

"Yes. That's what gives the Kragans an entirely different semantic orientation. For instance, they have nothing like a subject-predicate sentence structure. That's why, Stanley-Browne to the contrary notwithstanding, they are entirely non-religious. Their language hasn't instilled in them a predisposition to think of everything as the result of an action performed by an agent. And they have no definite parts of speech; any word can be used as any part of speech, depending on context. Tense is applied to words used as nouns, not words used as verbs; there are four tenses—spatial-temporal present, things here-and-now; spatial present and temporal remote, things which were here at some other time; spatial remote and temporal present, things existing now somewhere else, and spatial-temporal remote, things somewhere else some other time."

"Why, it's a wonder they haven't developed a Theory of Relativity!"

"They have. It resembles ours about the way the Wright Brothers' airplane resembles this aircar, but I was explaining the Keene-Gonzales-Dillingham Theory and the older Einstein Theory to King Kankad once, and it was beautiful to watch how he picked it up. Half the time, he was a jump ahead of me."

The aircar began losing altitude and speed as they came in over Kraggork Swamp; the treetops below blended into a level plain of yellow-green, pierced by glints of stagnant water underneath and broken by an occasional low hillock, sometimes topped by a stockaded village.

"Those are the swamp-savages' homes," he told her. "Most of what you find in Stanley-Browne about them is fairly accurate. He spent a lot of time among them. He never seems to have realized, though, that they are living now as they have ever since the first appearance of intelligent life on this planet."

"You mean, they're the real aboriginal people of Uller?"

"They and the Jeel cannibals, whom we are doing our best to exterminate," he replied. "You see, at one time, the dominant type of mobile land-life was the

thing we call a shellosaur, a big thing, running from
five to fifteen tons, plated all over with silicate shell,
till it looked like a six-legged pine-cone. Some were
herbivores and some were carnivores. There are a few
left, in remote places—quite a few in the Southern
Hemisphere, which we haven't explored very much.
They were a satisfied life-form. Outside of a volcano
or an earthquake or an avalanche, nothing could hurt
a shellosaur but a bigger shellosaur.

"Finally, of course, they grew beyond their suste-
nance-limit, but in the meantime, some of them began
specializing on mobility instead of armor and began
excreting waste-matter instead of turning it to shell.
Some of these new species got rid of their shell entirely. *Parahomo sapiens Ulleris* is descended from
one of these.

"The shellosaurs were still a serious menace,
though. The ancestors of the present Ulleran, the proto-
geeks, when they were at about the Java Ape-Man
stage of development, took two divergent courses to
escape the shellosaurs. Some of them took to the
swamps, where the shellosaurs would sink if they tried
to follow. Those savages, down there, are still living
in the same manner; they never progressed. Others
encountered problems of survival which had to be
overcome by invention. They progressed to barba-
rism, like the people of the fishing-villages, and some
of them progressed to civilization, like the Konkrookans and the Keegarkans.

"Then, there were others who took to the high
rocks, where the shellosaurs couldn't climb. The Jeels
are the primitive, original example of that. Most of
the North Uller civilizations developed from moun-
taineer-savages, and so did the Zirks and the other
northern plains nomads."

"Well, how about the Kragans?" Paula asked. "Which were they?"

Von Schlichten was scanning the horizon ahead. He pulled over a pair of fifty-power binoculars on a swinging arm and put them where she could use them.

"Right ahead, there; just a little to the left. See that brown-gray spot on the landward edge of the swamp? That's King Kankad's Town. It's been there for thousands of years, and it's always been Kankad's Town. You might say, even the same Kankad. The Kragan kings have always provided their own heirs, by self-fertilization. That's a complicated process, involving simultaneous male and female masturbation, but the offspring is an exact duplicate of the single parent. The present Kankad speaks of his heir as 'Little Me,' which is a fairly accurate way of putting it."

He knew what she was seeing through the glasses— a massive butte of flint, jutting out into the swamp on the end of a sharp ridge, with a city on top of it. All the buildings were multi-storied, some piling upward from the top and some clinging to the sides. The high watchtower at the front now carried a telecast-director, aimed at an automatic relay-station on an unmanned orbiter two thousand miles off-planet.

"They're either swamp-people who moved up onto that rock, or they're mountaineers who came out that far along the ridge and stopped," she said. "Which?"

"Nobody's ever tried to find out. Maybe if you stay on Uller long enough, you can. That ought to be good for about eight to ten honorary doctorates. And maybe a hundred sols a year in book royalties."

"Maybe I'll just do that, general. . . . What's that, on the little island over there?" she asked, shifting the glasses. "A clump of flat-roofed buildings. Under a red-and-yellow danger-flag."

"That's Dynamite Island; the Kragans have an explosives-plant there. They make nitroglycerine, like all the thalassic peoples; they also make TNT and catastrophite, and propellants. Learned that from us, of course. They also manufacture most of their own firearms, some of them pretty extreme—up to 25-mm for shoulder rifles. Don't ever fire one; it'd break every bone in your body."

"Are they that much stronger than us?"

He shook his head. "Just denser, heavier. They're about equal to us in weight-lifting. They can't run, or jump, as well as we can. We often come out here for games with the Kragans, where the geeks can't watch us. And that reminds me—you're right about that being a term of derogation, because I don't believe I've ever knowingly spoken of a Kragan as a geek, and in fact they've picked up the word from us and apply it to all non-Kragans. But as I was saying, our baseball team has to give theirs a handicap, but their football team can beat the daylights out of ours. In a tug-of-war, we have to put two men on our end for every one of theirs. But they don't even try to play tennis with us."

"Don't the other natives make their own firearms?"

"No, and we're not going to teach them how. The thalassic peoples here in the Equatorial Zone are fairly good empirical, teaspoon-measure, chemists. Well, no, alchemists. They found out how to make nitroglycerine, and use it for blasting and for bombs and mines, and they screw little capsules of it on the ends of their arrows. Most of their chemistry, such as it is, was learned in trying to prevent organic materials, like wood, from petrifying. Up in the north, where it gets cold, they learned a lot about metallurgy and ceramics, and about forced-draft pneumatics, from

having to keep fires going all winter to thaw frozen
food. They make air-rifles, to shoot metal darts."

The aircar came in, circling slowly over the town
on the big rock, and let down on the roof of the castle-
like building from which the watchtower rose. There
were a dozen or so individuals waiting for them—the
five Terrans, three men and two women, from the
telecast station, and the rest Kragans. One of these,
dark-skinned but with speckles no darker than light
amber, armed only with a heavy dagger, came over
and clapped von Schlichten on the shoulder, grinning
opalescently.

"Greetings, Von!" he squawked in Kragan, then,
seeing Paula, switched over to the customary language
of the Takkad Sea country. "It makes happiness to
see you. How long will you stay with us?"

"Till the *Aldebaran* gets in from Konkrook, to pick
up the rifles," von Schlichten replied, in Lingua Terra.
He looked at his watch. "Two hours and a
half . . . Kankad, this is Paula Quinton; Paula, King
Kankad."

He took out his geek-speaker and crammed it into
his mouth. Before any other race on Uller, that would
have been the most shocking sort of bad manners,
without the token-concealment of the handkerchief.
Kankad took it as a matter of course. At some length,
von Schlichten explained the nature of Paula's sociographic work, her connection with the Extraterrestrials' Rights Association, and her intention of going to
the Arctic mines. Kankad nodded.

"You were right," he said. "I wouldn't have understood all that in your language. If I had read it, maybe,
but not if I heard it." He put his upper right hand on
Paula's shoulder and uttered a clicking approximation
of her name. "I make you one of us," he told her.

"You must come back, after the work stops at the mines; if you want to learn about my people, I'll show you what you want to see, and tell you what you want to know. But why not stay here? Why bother about those geeks at the mines; the Company treats them much better than they deserve. Stay here with us; we will make you happy to be with us."

Paula replied slowly: "I thank Kankad, but I must go. Those on Terra who sent me here want me to learn for myself how the workers at the mines are treated. But I will come back—in a hundred, a hundred and fifty days."

Kankad's opal-jeweled grin widened. "Good! We'll be waiting for you." He turned and introduced another Kragan, about his own age, who wore the equipment and insignia of a Company native-major and was freshly painted with the Company emblem. "This is Kormork. He and I have borne young to each other. Kormork, you watch over Paula Quinton." He managed, on the second try, to make it more or less recognizable. "Bring her back safe. Or else find yourself a good place to hide."

Kankad introduced the rest of his people, and von Schlichten introduced the Terrans from the telecast-station. Then Kankad looked at the watch he was wearing on his lower left wrist.

"We will have plenty of time, before the ship comes, to show Paula the town," he suggested. "Von, you know better than I do what she would like to see."

He led the way past a pair of long 90-mm guns to a stone stairway. Von Schlichten explained, as they went down, that the guns of King Kankad's Town were the only artillery above 75-mm on Uller in non-Terran hands. They climbed into an open machine-gun carrier and strapped themselves to their seats, and for two hours King Kankad showed her the sights of the town. They visited the school, where young Kragans were being taught to read Lingua Terra and studied from textbooks printed in Johannesburg and Sydney and Buenos Aires. Kankad showed her the repairshops, where two-score descendants of Kragan rieverchieftains were working on contragravity equipment, under the supervision of a Scottish-Afrikander and his Malay-Portuguese wife; the small-arms factory, where very respectable copies of Terran rifles and pistols and auto-weapons were being turned out; the machineshop; the physics and chemistry labs; the hospital; the ammunition-loading plant; the battery of 155-mm Long Toms, built in Kankad's own shops, which covered the road up the sloping rock-spine behind the city; the printing-shop and book-bindery; the observatory, with a big telescope and an ingenious orrery of the Beta Hydrae system; the nuclear-power plant, part of the original price for giving up brigandage.

Half an hour before the ship from Konkrook was due, they had arrived at the airport, where a gang of Kragans were clearing a berth for the *Aldebaran*. From somewhere, Kankad produced two cold bottles of Cape Town beer for Paula and von Schlichten, and a bowl of some boiling-hot black liquid for himself. Von Schlichten and Paula lit cigarettes; between sips of his bubbling hell-brew, Kankad gnawed on the stalk of some swamp-plant. Paula seemed as much surprised at Kankad's disregard for the eating taboo as she had been at von Schlichten's open flouting of the convention of concealment when he had put in his geekspeaker.

"This is the only place on Uller where this happens," von Schlichten told her. "Here, or in the field when Terran and Kragan soldiers are together. There aren't any taboos between us and the Kragans."

"No," Kankad said. "We cannot eat each others' food, and because our bodies are different, we cannot be the fathers of each others' young. But we have been battle-comrades, and worksharers, and we have learned from each other, my people more from yours than yours from mine. Before you came, my people were like children, shooting arrows at little animals on the beach, and climbing among the rocks at dare-me-and-I-do, and playing war with toy weapons. But we are growing up, and it will not be long before we will stand beside you, as the grown son stands beside his parent, and when that day comes, you will not be ashamed of us."

It was easy to forget that Kankad had four arms and a rubbery, quartz-speckled skin, and a face like a lizard.

"I have always wished that some of your people could come to Terra, to study," von Schlichten said. "I was talking about it with Sid Harrington, only a short while ago. He thinks it would be a good thing, for your people and for mine."

"Yes. I want Little Me, when he's old enough to travel, to visit your world," Kankad said. "And some of the other young ones. And when Little Me is old enough to take over the rule of our people, I would like to go to Terra, myself."

"Some day, I am going to return to Terra; I would like to have you make the trip with me," von Schlichten said.

"That would be wonderful, Von!" Kankad exclaimed. "I want to see your world, before I die. It must be a wonderful place. A world is what its people make it, and your people must be able to make anything of your world that you would want."

"We almost made a lifeless desert, like the poles of Uller, out of our world, once," von Schlichten told him. "Four hundred and more years ago, we fought great wars among ourselves, with weapons such as I hope will never even be thought of on Uller. Our whole Northern Hemisphere, where our greatest nations were, was devastated; much of it is wasteland to this day. But we put an end to that folly in time; we made one nation out of all our people, and swore never to commit such crimes again, and then we built the ships that took us out to the stars. But I want you to see our world, and some of the other worlds that we have visited, I think you would like it."

"I know I would. And with you to tell me what the things I would see meant. . . ." Kankad was silent for a moment. Then he spoke again, changing the subject abruptly.

"I hope Paula will pardon me, but isn't Paula the kind of Terran that bears young?"

"That's right, Kankad. I never bore any, yet, but that's the kind of Terran I am."

"I like Paula," Kankad said. "She has come all the way from Terra to help us, and to learn about us. Of course, the Kragans don't need that kind of help, and the geeks, who would stick a knife in her as soon as she turned her back on them, don't deserve it. But she wants to learn about us, just as I want to learn about Terra. Von, why don't you and Paula have young?" he asked. "I think that would be fine. Then, Little Paula-Von and Little Me could be friends, long after the three of us are dead and gone."

VI-

The Bad News Came
After the Coffee

The last clatter of silverware and dishes ceased as the native servants finished clearing the table. There was a remaining clatter of cups and saucers; liqueur-glasses tinkled, and an occasional cigarette-lighter clicked. At the head table, the voices seemed louder.

"...don't like it a millisol's worth," Brigadier-General Barney Mordkovitz, the Skilk military CO, was saying to the lady on his right. "They're too confounded meek. Nowadays, nobody yells *'Znidd suddabit!'* at you. Nobody sticks all four thumbs in his mouth and waves his fingers. Nobody commits nuisance on the sidewalk in front of you. They just stand and look at you like a farmer looking at a turkey the week before Christmas, and that I don't like!"

"Oh, bosh!" Jules Keaveney, the Skilk Resident-Agent, at the head of the table, exclaimed. "You soldiers are all alike—begging your pardon, General von Schlichten," he nodded in the direction of the guest of honor. "If they don't bow and scrape to you and get off the sidewalk to let you pass, you say they're insolent and need a lesson. If they do, you say they're plotting insurrection."

"What I said," Mordkovitz repeated, "was that I expect a certain amount of disorder, and a certain minimum show of hostility toward us from some of these geeks, to conform to what I know to be our unpopularity with many of them. When I don't find it, I want to know why."

"I'm inclined," von Schlichten came to his subordinate's support, "to agree. This sudden absence of overt hostility is disquieting. Colonel Cheng-Li," he called on the local Intelligence officer and Constabulary chief. "This fellow Rakkeed was here, about a month ago. Was there any noticeable disorder at that time? Anti-Terran demonstrations, attacks on Company property or personnel, shooting at aircars, that sort of thing?"

"No more than usual, general. In fact, it was when Rakkeed came here that the condition General Mordkovitz was speaking of began to become conspicuous. We did catch some of Rakkeed's disciples trying to get in among the enlisted men of the Tenth N.U.N.I. and the Fifth Zirk Cavalry and promote disaffection. That was reported at the time, sir."

"And acted upon, as far as the civil administration would permit," von Schlichten replied. "And I might say that Lieutenant-Governor Blount has reported from Keegark, where he is now, that the same unnatural absence of hostility exists there."

"Well, of course, general," Keaveney said patronizingly. "King Orgzild has things under pretty tight control at Keegark. He'd not allow a few fanatics to do anything to prejudice these spaceport negotiations."

"I wonder if the idea back of that spaceport proposition isn't to get us concentrated at Keegark, where Orgzild could wipe us all out in one surprise blow," somebody down the table suggested.

"Oh, Orgzild wouldn't be crazy enough to try anything like that," Commander Dirk Prinsloo, of the *Aldebaran,* declared. "He'd get away with it for just twelve months—the time it would take to get the news to Terra and for a Federation Space Navy task-force to get here. And then, there'd be little bits of radio-active geek floating around this system as far out as the orbit of Beta Hydrae VII."

"That's quite true," von Schlichten agreed. "The point is, does Orgzild know it? I doubt if he even believes there is a Terra."

"Then where in Space does he think we come from?" Keaveney demanded.

"I believe he thinks Niflheim is our home world," von Schlichten replied. "Or, rather, the string of or-biters and artificial satellites around Niflheim. Where he thinks Niflheim is, I wouldn't even try to guess."

"Well, it takes six months for a ship to go between here and Nif," Prinsloo considered. "Because of the hyperdrive effects, the experienced time of the voy-age, inside the ship, is of the order of three weeks. Taking that as the figure, he'd estimate the distance at about a quarter-million miles, assuming the velocity as being the speed of one of our contragravity-ships here on Uller. I'm assuming he doesn't even know there is a hyperdrive."

"Yes. After he'd wiped us out, he might even con-sider the idea of an invasion of Niflheim with captured contragravity ships," Hideyoshi O'Leary chuckled. "That would be a big laugh—if any of us were alive, then, to do any laughing."

"You don't really believe that, general?" Keaveney asked. His tone was still derisive, but under the deri-sion was uncertainty. After all, von Schlichten had been on Uller for fifteen years, to his two.

"Any question of geek psychology is wide open as far as I'm concerned; the longer I stay here, the less I understand it." Von Schlichten finished his brandy and got out cigarette-case and lighter. "I have an idea of the sort of garbled reports these spies of his who spend a year on Niflheim as laborers bring back."

"You know the line Rakkeed's been taking, of course," Colonel Cheng-Li put in. "He as much as says that Niflheim's our home, and that the farms where we raise food here, and those evergreen plantings on Konk Isthmus and between here and Grank are the beginning of an attempt to drive all native life from this planet and make it over for ourselves."

"And that savage didn't think an idea like that up for himself; he got it from somebody like Orgzild," the black-bearded brigadier-general added. "You know, the main base off Niflheim is practically self-supporting, with hydroponic-gardens and animal-tissue culture vats. And it's enough bigger than one of the *City* ships to pass for a little world. Yes, somebody like Orgzild, or King Firkked here, could easily pick up the idea that that's our home planet."

"But King Kankad was talking about..." Paula Quinton began.

"We were speaking of geeks, not Kragans." Von Schlichten lit his cigarette and held his lighter for hers. "You saw that big Beta Hydrae orrery at Kankad's observatory. Well, there's quite a little story about that. You know, it's generally realized by the natives here that Uller is a globe. The North Zirks have ridden all the way around it, on hipposaur-back, in the high latitudes, and the thalassic peoples at the Equator have sailed all the five equatorial seas and portaged all the isthmuses between. But, of course, Uller is the center of the universe; the sun travels around it, on a rather complicated double-spiral track. As a theory, it explains most of what they're able to observe, and any minor effects that don't conform to it are just ignored.

They have a model, a most ingenious affair run by clockwork, at the University of Konkrook, to show the apparent movement and position of Beta Hydrae in the sky; it does so fairly accurately.

"Well, some of our astronomers constructed this orrery, and exhibited it to a gathering of the leading native scholars, who are also the high-priests of the local religion. Sort of combined Academy of Arts and Sciences and College of Cardinals. They almost were massacred. As soon as the assembled pundits saw this thing and grasped its meaning, they began geeking and skreeking and yorking and squawking and brandishing knives—it was blasphemous, and sacrilegious, and undermined the Faith, and invalidated the whole logic-system.

"I was brigadier-general, in command of Konkrook military district, then—the post Them M'zangwe has now. When I got a riot-call from the University, I hustled around with a company of Kragans, and we cleared the hall with the bayonet and ran the reverend professors out onto the campus, and after we got things in hand, the Kragans crowded around the orrery, trying to set it up to show the existing position of the planet relative to the primary and figure out the theory back of it. They were very much interested; some of them must have sent word home about it, because Kankad came in on the next ship, wanting to see it. He was so much taken with it that Sid Harrington gave it to him. It's one of his most cherished possessions, but the Konkrook pundits bite all four thumbs and wave their fingers every time they think of it." He warmed his coffee from a controlled-temperature pot. "You can't use Kragan thinking on any subject as a criterion of what somebody like Orgzild's opinions will be."

"I never could understand the admiration some of

you military people have for those cutthroats," Keaveney declared. "Oh, yes, I can. You like them because they do your dirty work for you."

"He reads Stanley-Browne, too, I'll bet," Hideyoshi O'Leary said. "Miss Quinton, how did you like your visit to Kankad's Town? Still think the Kragans are cultural mongrels?"

"Why, they're wonderful! I never expected anything like it. They just seem to have picked up everything they could from us, and then gone on from there to develop a culture of their own with our techniques. For instance, those big guns, the ones they call the Ridge Battery, that they built for themselves. They aren't copies of Terran guns. They don't look like our work, or give you the feel our work would. And that telescope at the observatory," she continued. "Did they build that, too?"

"Yes, all we furnished was a couple of textbooks on lens-grinding and telescope-design, and a book on optics. You see, when we made that deal with them, they realized that we weren't any better fighters than they were; we just had better weapons. To have the same kind of weapons, they'd have to learn to make them, and once they began studying technology, they found that they had to study science. Weapon-making was the entering-wedge; after that, they found that they could use the same skills to make anything else they wanted. Give them another century or so and they'll be one of the great races of the galaxy."

"Yes, and it's a good thing they're our friends, too," Mordkovitz added. "I'm only sorry there are so few of them, and so many of the geeks."

"Yes, the Company ought to let us stockpile nuclear weapons here, just to be on the safe side," another officer, farther down the table, said.

"Well, I'm not exactly in favor of that," von Schlichten replied. "It's the same principle as not allowing guards who have to go in among the convicts to carry firearms. If somebody like Orgzild got hold of a nuclear bomb, even a little old First-Century H-bomb, he could use it for a model and construct a hundred like it, with all the plutonium we've been handing out for power reactors. And there are too few of us, and we're concentrated in too few places, to last long if that happened. What this planet needs, though, is a visit by a fifty-odd-ship task-force of the Space Navy, just to show the geeks what we have back of us. After a show like that, there'd be a lot less *znidd suddabit* around here."

"General, I deplore that sort of talk," Keaveney said. "I hear too much of this mailed-fist-and-rattling-saber stuff from some of the junior officers here, without your giving countenance and encouragement to it. We're here to earn dividends for the stockholders of the Uller Company, and we can only do that by gaining the friendship, respect and confidence of the natives...."

"Mr. Keaveney," Paula Quinton spoke up. "I doubt if even you would seriously accuse the Extraterrestrials' Rights Association of favoring what you call a mailed-fist-and-rattling-saber policy. We've done everything in our power to help these people, and if anybody should have their friendship, we should. Well, only five days ago, in Konkrook, Mr. Mohammed Ferriera and I were attacked by a mob, our native aircar driver was murdered, and if it hadn't been for General von Schlichten and his soldiers, we'd have lost our own lives. Mr. Ferriera is still hospitalized as a result of injuries he received. It seems that General von Schlichten and his Kragans aren't trying to get friendship and confidence; they're willing to settle for respect, in the only way they can get it—by hitting harder and quicker than the geeks can."

Somebody down the table—one of the military, of course—said, "Hear, hear!" Von Schlichten came as close as a man wearing a monocle can to winking at Paula. Good girl, he thought; she's started playing on the Army team!

"Well, of course..." Keaveney began. Then he stopped, as a Terran sergeant came up to the table and bent over Barney Mordkovitz' shoulder, whispering urgently. The black-bearded brigadier rose immediately, taking his belt from the back of his chair and putting it on. Motioning the sergeant to accompany him, he spoke briefly to Keaveney and then came around the table to where von Schlichten sat, the Resident-Agent accompanying him.

"Message just came in from Konkrook, general," he said softly. "Sid Harrington's dead."

It took von Schlichten all of a second to grasp what had been said. "Good God! When? How?"

"Here's all we know, sir," the sergeant said, giving him a radioprint slip. "Came in ten minutes ago."

It was an all-station priority telecast. Governor-General Harrington had died suddenly, in his room, at 2210; there were no details. He glanced at his watch; it was 2243. Konkrook and Skilk were in the same time-zone; that was fast work. He handed the slip to Mordkovitz, who gave it to Keaveney.

"You from the telecast station, sergeant?" he asked. "All right, let's go."

"Wait a minute, general." Keaveney put out a hand to detain him as he took his belt and put it on. "How about this?" He gestured nervously with the radioprint slip.

"Get up and make an announcement, now," von Schlichten told him, fastening the buckle and hitching his pistol and survival-kit into place. "It'll be out all over the planet in half an hour. Never hold news out unnecessarily." He stubbed out his cigarette. "Come on, sergeant."

As he hurried from the banquet-room, he could hear Keaveney tapping on his wine-glass.

"Everybody, please! Let me have your attention! There has just come in a piece of the most tragic news. . . ."

VII -

Bismillah!
How Dumb Can We Get?

The lights had come on inside the semicircular and now open storm-porch of Company House, but it was still daylight outside. The sky above the mountain to the west was fading from crimson to burnt-orange, and a couple of the brighter stars were winking into visibility. Von Schlichten and the sergeant hurried a hundred yards down the street between low, thick-walled office buildings to the telecast station, next to the Administration Building.

A woman captain met him just inside the door of the big soundproofed room.

"We have a wavelength open to Konkrook, general," she said. "In booth three."

He nodded. "Thank you, captain. . . . We've all lost a true friend, haven't we?"

Another girl, a tech-sergeant, was in the booth; on the screen was the image of a third young woman, a lieutenant, at Konkrook station. The sergeant rose and started to leave the booth.

"Stick around, sergeant," von Schlichten told her. "I'll want you to take over when I'm through." He sat down in front of the combination visiscreen and pickup. "Now, lieutenant, just what happened?" he asked. "How did he die?"

"We think it was poison, general. General M'zangwe has ordered autopsy and chemical analysis.

If you can wait about ten minutes, he'll be able to talk to you, himself."

"Call him. In the meantime, give me everything you know."

"Well, the governor decided to go to bed early; he was going hunting in the morning. I suppose you know his usual routine?"

Von Schlichten nodded. Harrington would have taken a shower, put on his dressing-gown, and then sat down at his desk, lighted his pipe, poured a drink of Terran bourbon, and begun to write his diary.

"Well, at 2210, give or take a couple of minutes, the Kragan guard-sergeant on that floor heard ten pistol-shots, as fast as they could be fired semi-auto, in the governor's room. The door was locked, but he shot it off with his own pistol and went in. He found Governor Harrington on the floor, wearing only his gown, holding an empty pistol. He was in convulsions, frothing at the mouth, in horrible pain. Evidently he'd fired his pistol, which he kept on his desk, to call help; all the bullets had gone into the ceiling. The sergeant punched the emergency button, beside the bed, and reported, then tried to help the governor, but it was too late. One of the medics got there in five minutes, just as he was dying. He'd written his diary up to noon of today, and broken off in the middle of a word. There was a bottle and an overturned glass on his desk. The Constabulary got there a few minutes later, and then Brigadier-General M'zangwe took charge. A white rat, given fifteen drops from the whiskey-bottle, died with the same symptoms in about ninety seconds."

"Who had access to the whiskey-bottle?"

"A geek servant, who takes care of the room. He was caught, an hour earlier, trying to slip off the island without a pass; they were holding him at the guardhouse when Governor Harrington died. He's now being questioned by the Kragans." The girl's face was bleakly remorseless. "I hope they do plenty to him!"

"I hope they don't kill him before he talks."

"Wait a moment, general; we have General M'zangwe, now," the girl said. "I'll switch you over."

The screen broke into a kaleidoscopic jumble of color, then cleared; the chocolate-brown face of Themistocles M'zangwe was looking out of it.

"I heard what happened, how they found him, and about that geek chamber-valet being arrested," von Schlichten said. "Did you get anything out of him?"

"He's admitted putting poison in the bottle, but he claims it was his own idea. But he's one of Father Keeluk's parishioners, so . . ."

"Keeluk! God damn, so that was it!" von Schlichten almost shouted. "Now I know what he wanted with Stalin, and that goat, and those rabbits!"

Five thousand miles away, in Konkrook, Themistocles M'zangwe whistled.

"*Bismillah!* How dumb can we get?" he cried. "Of course they'd need terrestrial animals, to find out what would poison a Terran! Wait a minute; I'll make a note of that, to spring on this geek, if the Kragans haven't finished him by now." Von Schlichten watched M'zangwe pick up a stenophone and whisper into it for a moment. "All right, Carlos, what else?"

"Has Eric been notified?"

"We called Keegark, but he's in audience with King Orgzild, and we can't reach him."

"Well, who's in charge at Konkrook, now?"

"Not much of anybody. Laviola, the Fiscal Secretary, and Hans Meyerstein, the Banking Cartel's lawyer, and Howlett, the Personnel Chief, and Buhrmann, the Commercial Secretary, have made up a sort of quadrumvirate and are trying to run things. I don't know what would happen if anything came up suddenly...." A blue-gray uniformed arm, with a major's cuff-braid, came into the screen, handing a slip of paper to M'zangwe; he took it, glanced at it, and swore. Von Schlichten waited until he had read it through.

"Well, something has, all right," the African said. "We just got a call from Jaikark's Palace—a revolt's broken out, presumably headed by Gurgurk; Household Guards either mutinied or wiped out by the mutineers, all but those twenty Kragan Rifles we loaned Jaikark. They, and about a dozen of Jaikark's courtiers and their personal retainers, are holding the approaches to the King's apartments. The native-lieutenant in charge of the Kragans just radioed in; says the situation is desperate."

"When a Kragan says that, he means damn near hopeless. Is this being recorded?" When M'zang nodded, he continued: "All right. Use the recording for your authority and take charge. I'm declaring martial rule at Konkrook, as of now, 2253. Tell Eric Blount what's happened, and what you've done, as soon as you can get in touch with him. I'm leaving for Konkrook at once; I ought to get in by 0800.

"Now, as to the trouble at the Palace. Don't commit more than one company of Kragans and ten airjeeps and four combat-cars, and tell them to evacuate Jaikark and his followers and our Kragans to Gongonk Island. And alert your whole force. These geek palace revolutions are always synchronized with street-rioting, and this thing seems to have been synchronized with Sid Harrington's death, too. Get our Kragans out if you can't save anybody else from the Palace, but sacrificing thirty or forty men to save twenty is no kind of business. And keep sending reports; I can pick them up on my car radio as I come down." He turned to the girl sergeant. "Keep on this; there'll be more coming in."

He rose and left the booth. If we can pull Jaikark's bacon off the fire, he was thinking, the Company can dictate its own terms to him afterward; if Jaikark's killed, we'll have Gurgurk's head off for it, and then take over Konkrook. In either case, it'll be a long step toward getting rid of all these geek despots. And with Eric Blount as Governor-General . . .

The girl captain in charge of the station met him as he came out.

"Poison," he told her. "A geek servant did the job, on orders from Gurgurk and possibly Rakkeed. Gurgurk's started a putsch against King Jaikark; I'm going to Konkrook at once. Call the military airport and have my command-car brought to Company House."

Harry Quong and Hassan Bogdanoff had been at the banquet, too; on a world of lizard-faced silicate-eaters, the social difference between a human general and a human aircar-driver was almost infinitesimal. He'd have to talk to Barney Mordkovitz, too; when word of events at Konkrook got out among the local geeks, as it probably had already . . .

The inner door of the soundproofed telecast-room burst open, three men hurried inside, and it slammed shut behind them. In the brief interval, there had been firing audible from outside. One of the men had a pistol in his right hand, and with his left arm he supported a companion, whose shoulder was mangled and dripped blood. The third man had a burp-gun in his hands. All were in civilian dress—shorts and light jackets. The man with the pistol holstered it and helped his injured companion into a chair. The burp-gunner advanced into the room, looked around, saw von Schlichten, and addressed him.

"General! The geeks turned on us!" he cried. "The Tenth North Uller's mutinied; they're running wild all over the place. They've taken their barracks and supply-buildings, and the lorry-hangars and the maintenance-yard; they're headed this way in a mob. Some of the Zirk Cavalry's joined them."

"How about the Kragans?"

"The Eighteenth Rifles? They're with us. I saw a party of them firing into the mob; I saw some of the Tenth N.U.N.I. tossing a dead Kragan on their bayonets. . . ."

"Have any ammo left for that burp-gun? Come on, then; let's see what it's like at Company House," von Schlichten said. "Captain Malavez, you know what to do about defending this station. Get busy doing it. And have that girl in booth three tell Konkrook what's happened here, and say that I won't be coming down, as planned, just yet."

He opened the door, and the rattle of shots outside became audible again. The civilian with the burp-gun knew better than to let a general go out first; elbowing von Schlichten out of the way, he crouched over his weapon and dashed outside. Drawing his pistol, von Schlichten followed, pulling the door shut after him.

Darkness had fallen, while he had been inside; now the whole Company Reservation was ablaze with electric lights. Somebody at the power-plant—either the regular staff, if they were still holding, or the mutineers, if they had taken it—had thrown on the emergency lights. There was a confused mass of gray-skinned figures in front of Company House, reflected light twinkling on steel over them; from the direction

of the native-troops barracks more natives were coming on the run. On the roof of a building across the
street, two machine-guns were already firing into the
mob. A group of Terrans came running out of a roadway between two buildings, from the direction of the
repair-shops; several of them paused to fire behind
them with pistols. They started toward Company
House, saw what was going on there, and veered,
darting into the door of the building from which the
auto-weapons were firing. From up the street, a
hundred-odd saurian-faced native soldiers were coming at the double, bayonets fixed and rifles at high
port; with them ran several Terrans. Motioning his
companion to follow, von Schlichten ran to meet them,
falling in beside a Terran captain who ran in front.

"What's the score, captain?" he asked.

"Tenth North Uller and the Fifth Cavalry have mutinied; so have these rag-tag Auxiliaries. That mob
down there's part of them." He was puffing under the
double effort of running and talking. "Whole thing
blew up in seconds; no chance to communicate with
anybody. . . ."

A Terran woman, in black slacks and an orange
sweater, ran across the street in front of them, pursued
by a group of enlisted "men" of the Tenth North Uller
Native Infantry, all shrieking *"Znidd suddabit!"* The
fugitive ran into a doorway across the street; before
her pursuers were aware of their danger, the Kragans
had swept over them. There was no shooting; the slim,
cruel-bladed bayonets did the work. From behind him,
as he ran, von Schlichten could hear Kragan voices
in a new cry: *"Znidd geek! Znidd geek!"*

The mob were swarming up onto the steps and into
the semi-rotunda of the storm-porch. There was shooting, which told him that some of the humans who had

been at the banquet were still alive. He wondered, half-sick, how many, and whether they could hold out till he could clear the doorway, and, most of all, he found himself thinking of Paula Quinton. Skidding to a stop within fifty yards of the mob, he flung out his arms crucifix-wise to halt the Kragans. Behind, he could hear the Terrans and native-officers shouting commands to form front.

"Give them one clip, reload, and then give them the bayonet!" he ordered. "Shove them off the steps and then clear the porch!"

"One clip, fire, and reload, at will!" somebody passed it on in Kragan.

The hundred rifles let go all at once, and for five seconds they poured a deafening two thousand rounds into the mutineers. There was some fire in reply; a Zirk corporal narrowly missed him with a pistol, he saw the captain's head fly apart when an explosive rifle-bullet hit him, and half a dozen Kragans went down.

"Reload! Set your safeties!" von Schlichten bellowed. "Charge!"

Under human officers, the North Uller Native Infantry would have stood firm. Even under their native-officers and sergeants, they should not have broken as they did, but the best of these had paid for their loyalty to the Company with their lives, and the rest had destroyed their authority by revolting against the source from which it was derived. At that, the Skilkan peasantry who made up the Tenth Infantry and the Zirk cavalrymen tried briefly to fight as individuals, shrieking *"Znidd suddabit!"* until the Kragans were upon them, stabbing and shooting. They drove the rioters from the steps or killed them there, they wiped out those who had gotten into the semicircle of the storm-porch. The inside doors, von Schlichten saw, were open, but beyond them were Terrans and a dozen or so Kragans. Hideyoshi O'Leary and Barney Mordkovitz seemed to be in command of these.

"We had about thirty seconds' warning," Mordkovitz reported, "and the Kragans in the hall bought us another sixty seconds. Of course, we all had our pistols. . . ."

"Hey! These storm-doors are wedged!" somebody discovered. "Those goddam geek servants . . . !"

"Yeah, kill any of them you catch," somebody else advised. "If we could have gotten these doors closed . . ."

The mob, driven from the steps, was trying to reform and renew the attack. From up the street, the machine-guns, silent during the bayonet-fight, began hammering again. The mob surged forward to get out of their fire, and were met by a rifle-blast and a hedge of bayonets at the steps; they surged back, and the machine-guns flailed them again. They started to rush the building from whence the automatic-fire came, and there was a fusillade and a shriek of *"Znidd geek!"* from up the street. They turned and fled in the direction from whence they had come, bullets scourging them from three directions at once.

For a moment, von Schlichten and the three Terrans and eighty-odd Kragans who had survived the fight stood on the steps, weapons poised, seeking more enemies. The machine-guns up the street stuttered a few short bursts and were silent. From behind, the beleaguered Terrans and their Kragan guards were emerging. He saw Jules Keaveney and his wife, Commander Prinsloo of the *Aldebaran*, Harry Quong and Bogdanoff. Ah, there she was! He heaved a breath of relief and waved to her.

The Kragans were already setting about their after-battle chores. About twenty of them spread out on guard; the others, by fours, went into the street, one covering with his rifle while the other three checked on their own casualties, used the short, leaf-shaped swords they carried to slash off the heads of enemy wounded, and collected weapons and ammunition. A couple of hundred more Kragans, led by Native-Major Kormork, the co-parent of young with King Kankad, came up at the double and stopped in front of Company House.

"We were in quarters, aboard the *Aldebaran* and in the guesthouse at the airport," Kormork reported. "We were attacked, fifteen minutes ago, by a mob. We took ten minutes beating them off, and five more getting here. I sent Native-Captain Zeerjeek and the rest of the force to retake the supply-depot and the shops and lorry hangars, which had been taken, and relieve the military airport, which is under attack."

There was still firing from the commercial airport and the smaller military airfield. Once there was a string of heavy explosions that sounded like 80-mm rockets.

"Good enough. I hope you didn't spread yourself out too thin. What's the situation at the commercial airport?"

"The two ships, the *Aldebaran* and the freighter *Northern Star,* are both safe," Kormork replied. "I saw them go on contragravity and rise to about a hundred feet."

"Whose crowd is that you have?" he asked the Terran lieutenant who had taken over command of the first force of Kragans.

"Company 6, Eighteenth Rifles, sir. We were on duty at the guardhouse; fighting broke out in the direction of the native barracks. A couple of runners from Captain Retief of Company 4 came in with word that he was being attacked by mutineers from the Tenth N.U.N.I. but that he was holding them back. So Captain Charbonneau, who was killed a few minutes ago, left a Terran lieutenant and a Kragan native-lieutenant and a couple of native-sergeants and thirty Kragans to hold the guardhouse, and brought the rest of us here."

Von Schlichten nodded. "You'd pass the military airport and the power-plant, wouldn't you?" he asked.

"Yes, sir. The military airport's holding out, and I saw the red-and-yellow danger-lights on the fence around the power-plant."

That meant the power-plant was, for the time, safe; somebody'd turned twenty thousand volts into the fence.

"All right. I'm setting up my command post at the telecast station, where the communication equipment is." He turned to the crowd that had come out onto the porch from inside. "Where's Colonel Cheng-Li?"

"Here, general." The Intelligence and Constabulary officer pushed through the crowd. "I was on the phone, talking to the military airport, the commercial airport, ordnance depot, spaceport, ship-docks and power-plant. All answer. I'm afraid Pop Goode, at the city power-plant, is done for; nobody answers there, but the TV-pickup is still on in the load-dispatcher's room, and the place is full of geeks. Colonel Jarman's coming here with a lorry to get combat-car crews; he's short-handed. Port-Captain Leavitt has all the native labor at the airport and spaceport herded into a repair dock; he's keeping them covered with the forward 90-mm gun of the *Northern Star*. Lorry-hangars, repair-shops and maintenance-yards don't answer."

"That's what I was going to ask you. Good enough. Harry Quong, Hassan Bogdanoff!"

His command-car crew front-and-centered.

"I want you to take Colonel O'Leary up, as soon as my car's brought here. . . . Hid, you go up and see what's going on. Drop flares where there isn't any light. And take a look at the native-labor camp and the equipment-park, south of the reservation. . . . Kormork, you take all your gang, and half these soldiers from the Eighteenth, here, and help clear the native-troops barracks. And don't bother taking any prisoners; we can't spare personnel to guard them."

Kormork grinned. The taking of prisoners had always been one of those irrational Terran customs which no Ulleran regarded with favor, or even comprehension.

VIII-

Authority of
Governor-General von Schlichten

There was fresh intelligence from Konkrook, by the time he returned to the telecast station. Mutiny had broken out there among the laborers and native troops, who outnumbered the Terrans and their Kragan mercenaries on Gongonk Island by five thousand to five hundred and fifteen hundred respectively. The attempt to relieve Jaikark's palace had been called off before the relief-force could be sent; there was heavy and confused fighting all over the island, and most of the combat contragravity and about half the Kragan Rifles had had to be committed to defend the Company farms across the Channel, on the mainland, south of the city. There had also been an urgent call for help from Colonel Rodolfo MacKinnon, in command of Company troops at the Keegark Residency, and another from the Residency at Kwurk, one of the Free Cities on the eastern shore of Takkad Sea.

He called Keegark; a girl, apparently one of the civilian telecast technicians, answered.

"We must have help, General von Schlichten," she told him. "The native troops, all but two hundred Kragans, have mutinied. They have everything here except Company House—docks, airport, everything. We're trying to hold out, but there are thousands of them. Our Takkad Native Infantry, soldiers of King

Orgzild's army, and townspeople. They all seem to
have firearms...."

"What happened to Eric Blount and your Resident-
Agent, Mr. Lemoyne?"

"We don't know. They were at the Palace, talking
to King Orgzild. We've tried to call the Palace, but
we can't get through, general, we must have help...."

A call came in, a few minutes later, from Krink,
five hundred miles to the northeast across the mountains; the Resident-Agent there, one Francis Xavier
Shapiro, reported rioting in the city and an attempted
palace-revolution against King Jonkvank, and that the
Residency was under attack. By way of variety, it
was the army of King Jonkvank that had mutinied;
the Sixth North Uller Native Infantry and the two
companies of Zirk cavalry at Krink were still loyal,
along with the Kragans.

There was a pattern to all this. Von Schlichten
stood staring at the big map, on the wall, showing the
Takkad Sea area at the Equatorial Zone, and the country north of it to the pole, the area of Uller occupied
by the Company. He was almost beginning to discern
the underlying logic of the past half-hour's events
when Keaveney, the Skilk Resident, blundered into
him in a half-daze.

"Sorry, general, didn't see you." His face was
ashen, and his jowls sagged. Von Schlichten wondered if there could be another spectacle so woe-be-
gone as a back-slapping extrovert with the bottom
knocked out of him. "My God, it's happening all over
Uller! Not just here at Skilk; everywhere where we
have a residency or a trading-station. Why, it's the
end of all of us!"

"It's not quite that bad, Mr. Keaveney." He looked
at his watch. It was now nearly an hour since the

native troops here at Skilk had mutinied. Insurrections
like this usually succeeded or failed in the first hour.
It was a little early to be certain, but he was beginning
to suspect that this one hadn't succeeded. "If we all
do our part, we'll come out of it all right," he told
Keaveney, more cheerfully than he felt, then turned
to ask Brigadier-General Mordkovitz how the fighting
was going at the native-troops barracks.

"Not badly, general. Colonel Jarman's got some
contragravity up and working. They blew out all four
of the Tenth N.U.N.I.'s barracks; the Tenth and the
Zirks are trying to defend the cavalry barracks. Some
of our Kragans managed to slip around behind the
cavalry stables. They're leading out hipposaurs, and
sniping at the rear of the cavalry barracks."

"That'll give us some cavalry of our own; a lot of
these Kragans are good riders. . . . How about the repair-shops and maintenance-yard and lorry-hangars?
I don't want these geeks getting hold of that equipment
and using it against us."

"Kormork's outfit are trying to take back the lorry-
hangars. Jarman's got a couple of airjeeps and a combat-car helping them."

". . . won't be one of us left by this time tomorrow,"
Keaveney was wailing, to Paula Quinton and another
woman. "And the Company is finished!"

"We'd better get him a drink, or a cup of coffee,
general," Mordkovitz suggested. "With a knockout-
drop in it."

Colonel Cheng-Li, the Intelligence officer, seemed
to have somewhat the same idea. He approached
Keaveney and tried to quiet him. At the same time,
a woman in black slacks and an orange sweater—the
one whose pursuers had been overrun by the Kragans

at the beginning of the fighting—approached von Schlichten.

"General, King Kankad's calling," she said. "He's on the screen in booth four."

"Right." To avoid any possibility of misunderstanding, he slipped his geek-speaker into his mouth before entering the booth. Kankad's face was looking out of the screen at him, with Phil Yamazaki, the telecast operator at Kankad's Town, standing behind him.

"Von!" The Kragan spoke almost as though in physical pain. "What can I do to help? I have twenty thousand of my people here who are capable of bearing arms, all with firearms, but I have transport for only five hundred. Where shall I send them?"

Von Schlichten thought quickly. Keegark was finished; the Residency stood in the middle of the city, surrounded by two hundred thousand of King Orgzild's troops and subjects. Since Ullerans were bisexual, the total population, less the senile, crippled, and very young, was the military potential. Sending Kankad's five hundred warriors and his meager contragravity there would be the same as shoveling them into a furnace. The people at Keegark would have to be written off, like the twenty Kragans at Jaikark's palace.

"Send them to Konkrook," he decided. "Them M'zangwe's in command, there; he'll need help to hold the Company farms. Maybe he can find additional transport for you. I'll call him."

"I'll send off what force I can, at once," Kankad promised. "How does it go with you at Skilk?"

"We're holding, so far," he replied. "Paula is with me, here; she sends her friendship."

Captain Inez Malavez, the woman officer in charge of the station, put her head into the booth.

"General! Immediate-urgency message from Colonel O'Leary," she said. "Native laborers from the mine-labor camp are pouring into the mine-equipment park. Colonel O'Leary's used all his rockets and MG-ammunition trying to stop them."

"Call you back, later," von Schlichten told Kankad. "I'll see what Them M'zangwe can do about transport; get what force you can started for Konkrook at once."

He left the booth, removing his geek-speaker. "Barney!" he called. "General Mordkovitz! Who's the ranking officer in direct contact with the Eighteenth Rifles? Major Falkenberg?"

"That's right."

"Well, tell him to get as many of his Kragans as he can spare down to the equipment-park." He turned to Inez Malavez. "You call Jarman; tell him what O'Leary reported, and tell him to get cracking on it. Tell him not to let those geeks get any of that equipment onto contragravity; knock it down as fast as they try to lift out with it. And tell him to see what he can do in the way of troop-carriers or lorries, to get Falkenberg's Rifles to the equipment-park. . . . How's business at the lorry-hangars and maintenance-yard?"

"Kormork's still working on that," the girl captain told him. "Nothing definite, yet."

In one corner of the big room, somebody had thumbtacked a ten-foot-square map of the Company area to the floor. Paula Quinton and Mrs. Jules Keaveney were on their knees beside it, pushing out handfuls of little pink and white pills that somebody had brought in two bottles from the dispensary across the road, each using a billiard-bridge. The girl in the orange sweater had a handful of scribbled notes, and was telling them where to push the pills. There were other objects on the map, too—pistol-cartridges, and cigarettes, and foil-wrapped food-concentrate wafers. Paula, seeing him, straightened.

"The pink are ours, general," she said. "The white are the geeks." Von Schlichten suppressed a grin; that was the second time he'd heard her use that word, this evening. "The cigarettes are airjeeps, the cartridges are combat-cars, and the wafers are lorries or troop-carriers."

"Not exactly regulation map-markers, but I've seen stranger things used....Captain Malavez!"

"Yes, sir?" The girl captain, rushing past, her hands full of teleprint-sheets, stopped in mid-stride.

"What we need," he told her, "is a big TV-screen, and a pickup mounted on some sort of a contragravity vehicle at about two to five thousand feet directly overhead, to give us an image of the whole area. Can do?"

"Can try, sir. We have an eight-foot circular screen that ought to do all right for two thousand feet. I'll implement that at once."

Going into a temporarily idle telecast booth, he called Konkrook. First he spoke to a civilian who chewed a dead cigar, and then he got Themistocles M'zangwe on the screen.

"How is it, now?" he asked.

"Getting a little better," the Graeco-African replied. "Half an hour ago, we were shooting geeks out the windows, here; now we have them contained between the spaceport and the native-troops and labor barracks, and down the east side of the island to the farms. We have the wire around the farms on the island electrified, and we're using almost all our combat contragravity to keep the farms on the mainland clear." He hesitated for a moment. "Did you hear about Eric and Lemoyne?"

Von Schlichten shook his head.

"We just got a call from Rodolfo MacKinnon. He took a couple of prisoners and made them talk. The whole party that were at Orgzild's palace were massacred. Some of them were lucky enough to get killed fighting. The geeks took Eric and Hendrik alive; rolled them in a puddle of thermoconcentrate fuel and set fire to them. When we can spare the contragravity, we're going to drop something on the Kee-geek embassy, over in town."

"Well, that was what I wanted to call you about— contragravity." He told M'zangwe about King Kankad's offer. "His crowd ought to be coming in in a couple of hours. What can you scrape up to send to Kankad's Town to airlift Kragans in?"

"Well, we have three hundred-and-fifty-foot guncutters, one 90-mm gun apiece. The *Elmoran*, the *Gaucho*, and the *Bushranger*. But they're not much as transports, and we need them here pretty badly. Then, we have five fertilizer and charcoal scows, and a lot of heavy transport lorries, and two one-eighty-foot pickup boats."

"How about the *Piet Joubert*?" von Schlichten asked. "She was due in Konkrook from the east about 1300 today, wasn't she?"

M'zangwe swore. "She got in, all right. But the geeks boarded her at the dock, within twenty minutes after things started. They tried to lift out with her, and the Channel Battery shot her down into Konkrook Channel, off the Fifty Sixth Street docks."

"Well, you couldn't let the geeks have her, to use against us. What do you hear from the other ships?"

"Procyon's at Grank; we haven't had any reports of any kind from there, which doesn't look so good. The *Northern Lights* is at Grank, too. The *Oom Paul Kruger* should have been at Bwork, in the east, when the gun went off. And the *Jan Smuts* and the *Christiaan De Wett* were both at Keegark; we can assume Orgzild has both of them."

"All right. I'm sending *Aldebaran* to Kankad's, to pick up more reenforcements for you."

"We can use them! And with *Aldebaran,* we ought to be able to take the offensive against the city by this time tomorrow. Anything else?"

"Not at the moment. I'll see about getting *Aldebaran* sent off, now."

Leaving the booth, he heard, above the clatter of communications-machines and hubbub of voices, Jules Keaveney arguing contentiously. Evidently Colonel Cheng-Li's efforts to drag the Resident out of his despondency had been an excessive success.

"But it's crazy! Not just here; everywhere on Uller!" Keaveney was saying. "How did they do it? They have no telecast equipment."

"You have me stopped, Jules," Mordkovitz was replying. "I know a lot of rich geeks have receiving sets, but no sending sets."

The pattern that had been tantalizing von Schlichten took visible shape in his mind. For a moment, he shelved the matter of the *Aldebaran.*

"They didn't need sending equipment, Barney," he said. "They used ours."

"What do you mean?" Keaveney challenged.

"Look what happened. Sid Harrington was poisoned in Konkrook. The news, of course, was sent out at once, as the geeks knew it would be, to every residency and trading-station on Uller, and that was the signal they'd agreed upon, probably months in advance. All they had to do was have that geek servant put poison in Harrington's whiskey, and we did the rest."

"Well, what was our intelligence doing—sleeping?" Keaveney demanded angrily.

"No, they were writing reports for your civil administration blokes to stuff in the wastebasket, and being called mailed-fist-and-rattling-saber alarmists for their pains." He turned away from Keaveney. "Barney, where's Dirk Prinsloo?"

"Aboard his ship. He hitched a ride to the airport with Jarman, when he was here picking up air-crews."

"Call him. Tell him to take the *Aldebaran* to Kankad's Town, at once; as soon as he arrives there, which ought to be about 1100, he's to pick up all the Kragans he can pack aboard and take them to Konkrook. From then on, he'll be under Them M'zangwe's orders."

"To Konkrook?" Keaveney fairly howled. "Are you nuts? Don't you think we need reenforcements here, too?"

"Yes, I do. I'm going to try to get them," von Schlichten told him. "Now pipe down and get out of people's way."

He crossed the room, to where two Kragans, a male sergeant, and the ubiquitous girl in the orange sweater were struggling to get a big circular TV-screen up, then turned to look at the situation-map. A girl tech-sergeant was keeping Paula Quinton and Mrs. Jules Keaveney informed.

"Start pushing geeks out of the Fifth Zirk Cavalry barracks," the sergeant was saying. "The one at the north end, and the one next to it; they're both on fire, now." She tossed a slip into the wastebasket beside her and glanced at the next slip. "And more pink pills back of the barracks and stables, and move them a little to the northwest; Kragans as skirmishers, to intercept geeks trying to slip away from the cavalry barracks."

"Though why we want to do that, I don't know," Mrs. Keaveney said, pushing out a handful of pink pills with her billiard-bridge. "Let them go, and good riddance!"

"I never did like this bridge-of-silver-for-a-fleeing-enemy idea," Paula Quinton said, evicting token-mutineers from the two northern barracks. "There's usually two-way traffic on bridges. Kill them here and we won't have to worry about keeping them out."

Of course, it was easy to be bloodthirsty about pink pills and white pills. Once, on a three-months' reaction-drive voyage from Yggdrasill to Loki, he had taught a couple of professors of extraterrestrial zoology to play *kriegspiel,* and before the end of the trip, he was being horrified by the callous disregard they showed for casualties. But little Paula had the right idea; dead enemies don't hit back.

A young Kragan with his lower left arm in a sling and a daub of antiseptic plaster over the back of his head came up and gave him a radioprint slip. Guido Karamessinis, the Resident-Agent at Grank, had reported, at last. The city, he said, was quiet, but King Yoorkerk's troops had seized the Company airport and docks, taken the *Procyon* and the *Northern Lights* and put guards aboard them, and were surrounding the Residency. He wanted to know what to do.

Von Schlichten managed to get him on the screen, after a while.

"It looks as though Yoorkerk's trying to play both sides at once," he told the Grank Resident. "If the rebellion's put down, he'll come forward as your friend and protector; if we're wiped out elsewhere, he'll yell *'Znidd suddabit!'* and swamp you. Don't antagonize him; we can't afford to fight this war on any more fronts than we are now. We'll try to do something to get you unfrozen, before long."

He called Krink again. A girl with red-gold hair and a dusting of freckles across her nose answered.

"How are you making out?" he asked.

"So far, fine, general. We're in complete control of the Company area, and all our native troops, not just the Kragans, are with us. Jonkvank's pushed the mutineers out of his palace, and we're keeping open a couple of streets between there and here. We air-lifted all our Kragans and half the Sixth N.U.N.I. to the Palace, and we have the Zirks patrolling the streets on 'saurback. Now, we have our lorries and troop-carriers out picking up elements of Jonkvank's loyal troops outside town."

"Who's doing the rioting, then?"

She named three of Jonkvank's regiments. "And the city hoodlums, and priests from the temples of one sect that followed Rakkeed, and Skilkan fifth columnists. Mr. Shapiro can give you the details. Shall I call him?"

"Never mind. He's probably busy, he's not as easy on the eyes as you are, and you're doing all right.... How long do you think it'd take, with the equipment you have, to airlift all of Jonkvank's loyal troops into the city?"

"Not before this time tomorrow."

"All right. Are you in radio communication with Jonkvank now?"

"Full telecast, audio-visual," the girl replied. "Just a minute, general."

He put in his geek-speaker. The screen exploded into multi-colored light, then cleared. Within a few minutes, a saurian Ulleran face was looking out of it at him—a harsh-lined, elderly face, with an old scar, quartz-crusted, along one side.

"Your Majesty," von Schlichten greeted him.

Jonkvank pronounced something intended to correspond to von Schlichten's name. "We have image-met under sad circumstances, general," he said.

"Sad for both of us, King Jonkvank; we must help one another. I am told that your soldiers in Krink have risen against you, and that your loyal troops are far from the city."

"Yes. That was the work of my War Minister, Hurkkurk, who was in the pay of King Firkked of Skilk, may Jeels devour him alive! I have Hurkkurk's head here somewhere, if you want to see it, but that will not bring my loyal soldiers to Krink any sooner."

"Dead traitors' heads do not interest me, King Jonkvank," von Schlichten replied, in what he estimated that the Krinkan king would interpret as a tone of cold-blooded cruelty. "There are too many traitors' heads still on traitors' shoulders.... What regiments are loyal to you, and where are they now?"

Jonkvank began naming regiments and locating them, all at minor provincial towns at least a hundred miles from Krink.

"Hurkkurk did his work well; I'm afraid you killed him too mercifully," von Schlichten said. "Well, I'm sending the *Northern Star* to Krink. She can only bring in one regiment at a trip, the way they're scattered; which one do you want first?"

Jonkvank's mouth, until now compressed grimly, parted in a gleaming smile. He made an exclamation of pleasure which sounded rather like a boy running along a picket fence with a stick.

"Good, general! Good!" he cried. "The first should be the regiment Murderers, at Furnk; they all have rifles like your soldiers. Have them brought to the Great Square, at the Palace here. And then, the regiment Fear-Makers, at Jeelznidd, and the regiment Corpse-Reapers, at . . ."

"Let that go until the Murderers are in," von Schlichten advised. "They're at Furnk, you say? I'll send the *Northern Star* there, directly."

"Oh, good, general! I will not soon forget this! And as soon as the work is finished here, I will send soldiers to help you at Skilk. There shall be a great pile of the heads of those who had part in this wickedness, both here and there!"

"Good. Now, if you will pardon me, I'll go to give the necessary orders. . . ."

As he left the booth, he saw Hideyoshi O'Leary in front of the situation-map, and hailed him.

"Harry and Hassan are getting the car re-ammoed; they dropped me off here. Want to come up with us and see the show?"

"No, I want you to go to Krink, as soon as Harry brings the car here again." He told O'Leary what he intended doing. "You'll probably have to go around ahead of the *Star* and alert these regiments. And as soon as things stabilize at Krink, prod Jonkvank into airlifting troops here. You're authorized, in my name, to promise Jonkvank that he can assume political control at Skilk, after we've stuffed Firkked's head in the dustbin."

Jules Keaveney, who always seemed to be where he wasn't wanted, heard that and fairly screamed.

"General von Schlichten! That is a political decision! You have no authority to make promises like that; that is a matter for the Governor-General, at least!"

"Well, as of now, and until a successor to Sid Harrington can be sent here from Terra, I'm Governor-General," von Schlichten told him, mentally thanking Keaveney for reminding him of the necessity for such a step. "Captain Malavez! You will send out an all-station telecast, immediately: Military Commander-in-Chief Carlos von Schlichten, being informed of the deaths of both Governor-General Harrington and Lieutenant-Governor Blount, assumes the duties of Governor-General, as of 0001 today." He turned to Keaveney. "Does that satisfy you?" he asked.

"No, it doesn't. You have no authority to assume a civil position of any sort, let alone the very highest position. . . ."

Von Schlichten unbuttoned his holster and took out his authority, letting Keaveney look into the muzzle of it.

"Here it is," he said. "If you're wise, don't make me appeal to it."

Keaveney shrugged. "I can't argue with that," he said. "But I don't fancy the Uller Company is going to be impressed by it."

"The Uller Company," von Schlichten replied, "is six and a half parsecs away. It takes a ship six months to get from here to Terra, and another six months to get back. A radio message takes a little over twenty-one years, each way." He holstered the pistol again. "You were bitching about how we needed reenforcements, a while ago. Well, here's where we have to reverse Clausewitz and use politics as an extension by other means of war."

"That brings up another question, general," one of Keaveney's subordinates said. "Can we hold out long enough for help to get here from Terra?"

"By the time help could reach us from Terra," von Schlichten replied, "we'll either have this revolt crushed, or there won't be a live Terran left on Uller." He felt a brief sadistic pleasure as he watched Keaveney's face sag in horror. "What do you think we'll live on, for a year?" he asked. "On this planet, there's not more than a three months' supply of any sort of food a human can eat. And the ships that'll be coming in until word of our plight can get to Terra won't bring enough to keep us going. We need the farms and livestock and the animal-tissue culture plant at Konkrook, and the farms at Krink and on the plateau back of Skilk, and we need peace and native labor to work them."

Nobody seemed to have anything to say after that, for a while. Then Keaveney suggested that the next ship was due in from Niflheim in three months, and that it could be used to evacuate all the Terrans on Uller.

"And I'll personally shoot any able-bodied Terran who tries to board that ship," von Schlichten promised. "Get this through your heads, all of you. We are going to break this rebellion, and we are going to hold Uller for the Company and the Terran Federation." He looked around him. "Now, get back to work, all of you," he told the group that had formed around him and Keaveney. "Miss Quinton, you just heard me order my adjutant, Colonel O'Leary, on detached duty to Krink. I want you to take over for him. You'll have rank and authority as colonel for the duration of this war."

She was thunderstruck. "But I know absolutely nothing about military matters. There must be a hundred people here who are better qualified than I am...."

"There are, and they all have jobs, and I'd have to find replacements for them, and replacements for the replacements. You won't leave any vacancy to be filled. And you'll learn, fast enough." He went over to the situation-map again, and looked at the arrangement of pink and white pills. "First of all, I want you to call Jarman, at the military airport, and have an airjeep and driver sent around here for me. I'm going up and have a look around. Barney, keep the show going while I'm out, and tell Colonel Quinton what it's all about."

IX -

Don't Push Them Anywhere
Put Them Back in the Bottle

He looked at his watch, and stood for a moment, pumping the stale air and tobacco-smoke of the telecast station out of his lungs, as the light airjeep let down into the street. Oh-one-fifteen—two hours and a half since the mutiny at the native-troops barracks had broken out. The Company reservation was still ablaze with lights, and over the roof of the hospital and dispensary and test-lab he could see the glare of the burning barracks. There was more fire-glare to the south, in the direction of the mine-equipment park and the mine-labor camp, and from that direction the bulk of the firing was to be heard.

The driver, a young lieutenant who seemed to be of predominantly Malayan and Polynesian blood, slid back the duraglass canopy for him to climb in, then snapped it into place when he had strapped himself into his seat.

"Can you handle the armament, sir?" he asked.

Von Schlichten nodded approvingly. Not a very flattering question, but the boy was right to make sure, before they started out.

"I've done it, once or twice," he understated. "Let's go; I want a look at what's going on down at the equipment-park and the labor-camp, first."

They lifted up, the driver turning the nose of the airjeep in the direction of the flames and explosions and magnesium-lights to the south and tapping his booster-button gently. The vehicle shot forward and came floating in over the scene of the fighting. The situation-map at the improvised headquarters had shown a mixture of pink and white pills in the mine-equipment park; something was going to have to be done about the lag in correcting it, for the area was entirely in the hands of loyal Company troops, and the mob of laborers and mutinous soldiers had been pushed back into the temporary camp where the workers had been gathered to await transportation to the Arctic. As he feared, the rioting workers, many of whom were trained to handle contragravity equipment, had managed to lift up a number of dump-trucks and powershovels and bulldozers, intending to use them as improvised air-tanks, but Jarman's combat-cars had gotten on the job promptly and all of these had been shot down and were lying in wreckage, mostly among the rows of parked mining-equipment.

From the labor-camp, a surprising volume of fire was being directed against the attack which had already started from the retaken equipment-park. This was just another evidence of the failure of Intelligence and the Constabulary—and consequently of himself—to anticipate the brewing storm. There was, of course, practically no chance of keeping Ullerans from having native weapons, swords, knives, even bows and air-rifles, and a certain number of Volund-made trade-quality automatic pistols could be expected, but most of the fire was coming from military rifles, and now and then he could see the furnace-like backflash of a recoilless rifle or a bazooka, or the steady flicker of a machine-gun. Even if a few of these weapons had been brought from the barracks by retreating Tenth Infantry or Fifth Cavalry mutineers, there were still too many.

Hovering above the fighting, aloof from it, he saw six long troop-carriers land and disgorge Kragan Rifles who had been released by the liquidation of resistance at the native-troops barracks. A little later, two air-tanks floated in, and then two more, going off contragravity and lumbering on treads to fire their 90-mm rifles. At the same time, combat-cars swooped in, banging away with their lighter auto-cannon and launching rockets. The titanium prefab-huts, set up to house the laborers and intended to be taken north with them for their stay on the polar desert, were simply wiped away. Among the wreckage, resistance was being blown out like the lights of a candelabrum. Push the white pills out, girls, he thought. Don't push them anywhere; put them back in the bottle. This year, there wouldn't be any mining done at the North Pole; next year, the stockholders'll be bitching about their dividend-checks. And a lot of new machine operators are going to have to be trained for next year's mining. If there is any mining, next year.

He took up the handphone and called HQ.

"Von Schlichten, what's the wavelength of the officer in command at the equipment-park?"

A voice at the telecast station furnished it; he punched it out.

"Von Schlichten, right overhead. That you, Major Falkenberg? Nice going, major, how are your casualties?"

"Not too bad. Twenty or thirty Kragans and loyal Skilkans, and eight Terrans killed, about as many wounded."

"Pretty good, considering what you're running into. Get many of your Kragans mounted on those hipposaurs?"

"About a hundred, a lot of 'saurs got shot, while

we were leading them out from the stables."

"Well, I can see geeks streaming away from the labor-camp, out the south end, going in the direction of the river. Use what cavalry you have on them, and what contragravity you can spare. I'll drop a few flares to show their position and direction."

Anticipating him, the driver turned the airjeep and started toward the dry Hoork River. Von Schlichten nodded approval and told him to release flares when over the fugitives.

"Right," Falkenberg replied. "I'll get on it at once, general."

"And start moving that mine-equipment up into the Company area. Some of we it can put into the air; the rest we can use to build barricades. None of it do we want the geeks getting hold of, and the equipment-park's outside our practical perimeter. I'll send people to help you move it."

"No need to do that, sir; I have about a hundred and fifty loyal North Ullerans—foremen, technicians, overseers—who can handle it."

"All right. Use your own judgment. Put the stuff back of the native-troops barracks, and between the power-plant and the Company office-buildings, and anywhere else you can." The lieutenant nudged him and pushed a couple of buttons on the dashboard.

"Here go the flares, now."

Immediately, a couple of airjeeps pounced in, to strafe the fleeing enemy. Somebody must have already been issuing orders on another wavelength; a number of Kragans, riding hipposaurs, were galloping into the light of the flares.

"Now, let's have a look at the native barracks and the maintenance-yards," he said. "And then, we'll make a circuit around the Reservation, about two or three miles out. I'm not happy about where Firkked's army is."

The driver looked at him. "I've been worrying about that, too, sir," he said. "I can't understand why he hasn't jumped us, already. I know it takes time to get one of these geek armies on the road, but..."

"He's hoping our native troops and the mine laborers will be able to wipe us out, themselves," von Schlichten said. "For the timidity and stupidity of our enemies, Allah make us truly thankful, amen. It's something no commander should depend on, but be glad when it happens. If Firkked had had a couple of regiments on hand outside the reservation to jump us as soon as the Tenth and the Zirks mutinied, he could have swamped us in twenty minutes and we'll all have had our throats cut by now."

There was nothing going on in the area between the native barracks and the mountains except some sporadic firing as small patrols of Kragans clashed with clumps of fleeing mutineers. All the barracks, even those of the Rifles, were burning; the red-and-yellow danger-lights around the power-plant and the water-works and the explosives magazines were still on. Most of the floodlights were still on, and there was still some fighting around the maintenance-yard. It looked as though the survivors of the Tenth N.U.N.I. were in a few small pockets which were being squeezed out.

There was nothing at all going on north of the Reservation; the countryside, by day a checkerboard of walled fields and small villages, was dark, except for a dim light, here and there, where the occupants of some farmhouse had been awakened by the noise of battle. The airjeep dropped lower, and the driver slid open the window beside him; von Schlichten could hear the grunts and snorts and squawks of farm-animals, similarly aroused.

Then, two miles east of the Reservation, he caught a new sound—the flowing, riverlike, murmur of something vast on the move.

"Hear that, lieutenant?" he asked. "Head for it, at about a thousand feet. When we're directly above it, let go some flares."

"Yes, sir." The younger man had lowered his voice to a whisper. "That's geek, headed for the Reservation."

"Maybe Firkked's army," von Schlichten thought aloud. "Or maybe a city mob."

"Not quite noisy enough for a mob, is it, sir?"

"A tired mob," von Schlichten told him. "They'd start out on a run, yelling *'Znidd Suddabit!'* By the time they got across the bridges to this side of the river, they'd be winded. They'd stop for a blow, and then they'd settle down to steady slogging to save their wind. Sometimes a mob like that's worse than a fresh mob. They get stubborn; they act more deliberately."

The noises were growing clearer, louder. He picked up the phone and punched the wavelength of the military airport.

"Von Schlichten, my compliments to Colonel Jarman. Tell him there's a geek mob, or possibly Firkked's regulars, on the main highway from Skilk, two miles east of the Reservation. Get some combat contragravity over here, at once. We'll light them up for you. And tell Colonel Jarman to start flying patrols up and down along the Hoork River; this may not be the only gang that's coming out to see us."

The sounds were directly below, now—the scuffing of horny-soled feet on the dirt road, the clink and rattle of slung weapons, the clicking and squeeking of Ulleran voices.

The lieutenant said, "Here go the flares, sir."

Von Schlichten shut his eyes, then opened them slowly. The driver, upon releasing the flares, had nosed up, banked, turned, and was coming in again, down the road toward the advancing column. Von Schlichten peered into his all-armament sight, his foot on the machine-gun pedal and his fingers on the rocket buttons. The highway below was jammed with geeks, and they were all stopped dead and staring upward, as though hypnotized by the lights. A second later, they had recovered and were shooting—not at the airjeep, but at the four globes of blazing magnesium. Then he had the close-packed mass of non-humanity in his sights; he tramped the pedal and began punching buttons. He still had four rockets left by the time the mob was behind him.

"All right, let's take another pass at them. Same direction."

The driver put the airjeep into a quick loop and came out of it in front of the mob, who now had their backs turned and were staring in the direction in which they had last seen the vehicle. Again, von Schlichten plowed them with rockets and harrowed them with his guns. Some of the Skilkans were trying to get over the high fences on either side of the road—really stockades of petrified tree-trunks. Others were firing, and this time they were shooting at the airjeep. It took one hit from a heavy shellosaur-rifle, and, immediately, the driver banked and turned away from the road.

"Dammit, why did you do that?" von Schlichten demanded, lifting his foot from the gun-pedal. "Are you afraid of the kind of popguns those geeks are using?"

"I am not afraid to risk my vehicle, or myself, sir," the lieutenant replied, with the extreme formality of a very junior officer chewing out a very senior one. "I am, however, afraid to risk my passenger. Generals are not expendable, sir; neither are they issued for use as clay pigeons."

He was right, of course. Von Schlichten admitted it. "I'm too old to play cowboy, like this," he said. "Back to the Reservation, telecast station."

Looking back over his shoulder, he saw eight or ten more flares alight, and the ground-flashes of exploding shells and rockets; the air above the road was sparkling with gun-flames. Jarman must have had some contragravity ready to be sent off on the instant.

While he had been out, somebody had gotten a TV-pickup mounted on a contragravity-lifter and run up to two thousand feet, on the end of a steel-tough tensilon mooring-line. The big circular screen was lit, showing the whole Company Reservation, with the surrounding countryside foreshortened by perspective to the distant lights of Skilk. The map had been taken up from the floor, and a big terrain-board had been brought in from the Chief Engineer's office and set up in its place. In front of the screen, Paula Quinton, Barney Mordkovitz, Colonel Cheng-Li, and, conspicuously silent, Jules Keaveney sat drinking coffee and munching sandwiches. Half a dozen Terrans, of both sexes, were working furiously to get the markers which replaced the pink and white pills placed on the board, and one of Captain Inez Malavez's non-coms,

with a headset, was getting combat reports directly
from the switchboard. Everything was clicking like
well-oiled machinery.

On the TV-screen, the Residency area was ablaze
with light, and so were the ship-docks, the airport and
spaceport, the shops, and the maintenance-yard. On
the terrain-board, the latter was now marked as completely in Company hands. The ruins of the native-
troops barracks were still burning, and there was a
twinkle of orange-red here and there among the ruins
of labor-camp. Much of the equipment for the polar
mines had already been shifted into defensible ground.
The rest of the circle was dark, except for the distant
lights of Skilk, where the nuclear power plant was
apparently still functioning in native hands.

Then, without warning, a spot of white light blazed
into being southeast of the Company area and southwest of Skilk, followed by another and another. Instantly, von Schlichten glanced up at the row of smaller
screens, and on one of them saw the view as picked
up by a patrolling airjeep.

The army of King Firkked of Skilk had finally put
in its appearance, coming in two columns, one south-
ward from Skilk and the other northward along the
west bank of the dry river. The former had crossed
over and joined the latter, about three miles south of
the Reservation. The scene in the screen was similar
to the one he had, himself, witnessed through his
armament-sight. The Skilkan regulars had been
marching in formation, some on the road and some
along parallel lanes and paths. They had the look of
trained and disciplined troops, but they had made the
same mistake as the rabble that had been shot up on
the north side of the Reservation. Unused to attack
from the air, they had all halted in place and were

gaping open-mouthed, their opal teeth gleaming in the white flare-light. However, before the aircar had passed over them, the lead company of one regiment, armed with Terran rifles, had begun firing.

In the big screen, it could be seen that Colonel Jarman had thrown most of his available contragravity at them, including the combat-cars, that had already started to form the second wave of the attack on the mob to the north. Other flares bloomed in the darkness, and the fiery trails of rockets curved downward to end in yellow flashes on the ground.

The airjeep with the pickup circled back; the troops on the road and in the adjoining fields had broken. The former were caught between the fences which made Ulleran roads such death-traps when under air-attack. The latter had dispersed, and were running away, individually and by squads; at first, it looked like a panic, but he could see officers signaling to the larger groups of fugitives to open out, apparently directing the flight. By this time, there were ten or twelve combat-cars and about twenty airjeeps at work. In the moving view from the pickup-jeep, he saw what looked like a 90-mm rocket land in the middle of a company that was still trying to defend itself with small-arms fire on the road, wiping out about half of them.

"Make the most of it, boys," Barney Mordkovitz, his mouth full of sandwich, was saying. "Heave it to them; you won't get another chance like that at those buggers."

"Why not?" Colonel Paula Quinton wanted to know. Her military education was progressing, but it still had a few gaps to fill in.

"The next time they're air-struck, they won't stay bunched," Mordkovitz replied. "A lot of them didn't stay bunched this time, if you noticed. And they'll keep out from between the fences."

In the large screen, a quick succession of gun-flashes leaped up from the direction of the Hoork River; shells began bursting over the scene of the attack. The screen tuned to the pickup on the airjeep went dead; in the big screen, there was a twinkling of falling fire. Almost at once, thirty or forty rocket-trails converged on the gun-position, and, for a moment, explosions burned like a bonfire.

"They had a 75-mm at the rear of the column," somebody called from the big switchboard. "Lieuten-ant Kalanang's jeep was hit; Lieutenant Vermaas is cutting in his pickup on the same wavelength."

The small screen lighted again. In the big screen, a cluster of magnesium-lights appeared above where the Skilkan gun had been; in the small screen, there was a stubbled grain-field, pocked with craters, and the bodies of fifteen or twenty natives, all rather badly mangled. An overturned and apparently destroyed 75-mm gun lay on its side.

Five or six fairly large fires had broken out, by this time, around the point of attack. Von Schlichten nodded approvingly.

"I was wondering how long it'd take somebody to think of that," he said. "Granaries and forage-stacks on some of these farms. They'll burn for half an hour, at least." He looked at his watch. "And by that time, it'll be daylight."

"As far as we know, that was the only 75-mm gun Firkked had," Colonel Cheng-Li said. "He has at least six, possibly ten, 40-mm's. It's a wonder we haven't seen anything of them."

"Well, there's no way of being sure," Jules Keaveney said, "but I have an idea they're all at or around the Palace. Firkked knows about how much contragravity we have. He's probably wondering why we aren't bombing him, now."

"He doesn't know we've sold the Palace to King Jonkvank for an army," von Schlichten said. "And that reminds me—how much contragravity could Firkked scrape together, for an attack on us? I've been expecting a geek *Luftwaffe* over here, at any moment."

Colonel Cheng-Li studied the smoking tip of his cigarette for a moment. "Well, Firkked owns, personally, three ten-passenger aircars, a thing like a troop-carrier that he transports some of his courtiers around in, four airjeeps armed with a pair of 15-mm machine-guns apiece, and two big lorries. There are possibly two hundred vehicles of all types in Skilk and the country around, but some of them are in the hands of natives friendly to us and or hostile to Firkked. I can get the exact figures from the Constabulary office at Company House."

"That's close enough," von Schlichten told him. "And there'll be oodles of thermoconcentrate-fuel, and blasting explosives. Colonel Quinton, suppose you call Ed Wallingsby, the Chief Engineer, right away; have him commissioned colonel. Tell him to get to work making this place secure against air attack; tell him to consult with Colonel Jarman. Tell him to get those geeks Leavitt has penned in the repair-dock at the airport and use them to dig slit-trenches and fill sandbags and so on. He can use Kragan limited-duty wounded to guard them. . . . Mr. Keaveney, you'll begin setting up something in the way of an ARP-organization. You'll have to get along on what nobody else wants. You will also consult with Colonel Jarman, and with Colonel Wallingsby. Better get started on it now. Just think of everything around here that could go wrong in case of an air attack, and try to do something about it in advance."

X -

The Geek Luftwaffe
and the Kragan Airlift

At 0245, an attack developed on the northwestern corner of the Reservation, in the direction of the explosives magazines. It turned out to be relatively trivial. Remnants of the mob that had been broken up by air attack on the road had gotten together and were making rushes in small bands, keeping well spread out. Beating them off took considerable ammunition, but it was accomplished with negligible casualties to the defenders. They finally stopped coming around daylight.

In the meantime, Themistocles M'zangwe called from Konkrook, appearing in the screen with his left arm in a freshly white sling.

"What the hell have you been doing to yourself?" von Schlichten wanted to know.

"Crossbow-bolt, about half an hour ago. A couple of inches lower and acting Brigadier-General Colbert'd have been talking to you, now, instead of me."

"Lucky it didn't have a nitro-capsule on the end. How are you making out? Have Kankad's people started coming in, yet?"

"Oh, yes, about six hundred of them have gotten in already, in the damnedest collection of vehicles you ever saw. Kankad must be using every scrap of contragravity he has; it's a regular airborne Dunkirk-in-reverse. Kankad sent word that he's coming here

in person, as soon as he has things organized at his
place. And the geeks here have scraped together an
air-force of their own—farm-lorries, aircars, that sort
of thing—and they're using them to bomb us here
and at the mainland farm, mostly with nitroglycerine.
We've shot down about twenty of them, but they're
still coming. They tried a boat-attack across the Channel; that's how I got this. We've been doing some
bombing, ourselves; we made a down payment for
Eric Blount and Hendrik Lemoyne. Took a fifty-ton
tank off a fuel-lorry, fitted it with a detonator, filled
it with thermoconcentrate, and ferried it over on the
Elmoran and dumped it on the Keegarkan Embassy.
It must have landed in the middle of the central court;
in about fifteen seconds, flames were coming out every
window in the place." His face became less jovial.
"We had something pretty bad happen here, too," he
said. "That Konkrook Fencibles rabble of Prince Jaiz-
erd's mutinied, along with the others; they got into
the hospital and butchered everybody in the place,
patients and staff. The Kragans got there too late to
save anybody, but they wiped out the Fencibles. Jaiz-
erd himself was the only one they took alive, and he
didn't stay that way very long."

"How are you making out with your Civil Administration crowd?"

M'zangwe grimaced. "I haven't had to put any of
them under actual arrest, so far, but we've had to keep
Buhrmann away from the communications equipment
by force. He wanted to call you up and chew you out
for not evacuating everybody in the north to Konkrook."

"Is he crazy?"

"No, just scared. He says you're going to get everybody on Uller massacred by detail, when you could

save Konkrook by bringing them all here."

"You tell him I'm going to hold this planet, not just one city. Tell him I have a sense of my duty to the Company and its stockholders, if he hasn't; put it in those terms and he may understand you."

"Yes, I'll try that out on Meyerstein, too. He's in a hell of a state about the losses the Banking Cartel are taking on this deal. . . . Well, I'll call you when there's anything new."

By 0330, it was daylight; the attacks against the northwest corner of the perimeter stopped entirely. Wallingsby had the three-hundred-odd Skilkan laborers at work; he had gathered up all the tarpaulin he could find, and had the two sewing-machines in the tentmaker's shop running on sandbags. Jules Keaveney, to von Schlichten's agreeable surprise, had taken hold of his ARP assignment, and was doing an efficient job in organizing for fire-fighting, damage-control and first aid. Colonel Jarman had his airjeeps and combat-cars working in ever-widening circles over the countryside, shooting up everything in sight that even looked like contragravity equipment. Some of these patrols had to be recalled, around 1030, when sporadic nuisance-sniping began from the side of the mountain to the west. And, along with everything else, Paula Quinton managed, along with her other work, to get a complete digest prepared of the situation elsewhere in the Terran-occupied parts of the planet.

The situation at Konkrook was brightening steadily. The second wave of Kankad's improvised airlift, reenforced by contragravity from Konkrook, had come in; there were now close to two thousand fresh Kragans on Gongonk Island and the mainland farms, Kankad himself with them. The *Aldebaran* had reached Kankad's Town, and was loading another thousand

Kragans. . . .There was nothing more from Keegark. A message from Colonel MacKinnon had come in at dawn, to the effect that the geeks had penetrated his last defenses and that he was about to blow up the Residency; thereafter Keegark went off the air. . . . By 0730, the *Northern Star* had landed the regiment Murderers, armed with first-quality Terran infantry-rifles and a few machine-guns and bazookas, at the Palace at Krink, and by 0845 she had returned with another regiment, the Jeel-Feeders. The three-street lane connecting the Palace and the Residency had been widened to six, and then to eight. . . . Guido Karamessinis, at Grank, was still at uneasy peace with King Yoorkerk, who was still undecided whether the rebels or the Company were going to be the eventual victors, and afraid to take any irrevocable step in either direction. . . . Eight men and four women, the survivors of a trading-station on the eastern shore of Takkad Sea, reached Konkrook in a lorry; another trading station, on the south shore, reported by telecast that the natives there had refused to rise against them, and had crucified five of Rakkeed's disciples who had come among them preaching *znidd suddabit*.

At 1100, Paula Quinton and Barney Mordkovitz virtually ordered him to get some sleep. He went to his quarters at Company House, downed a spaceship-captain's-size drink of honey-rum, and slept until 1600. As he dressed and shaved, he could hear, through the open window, the slow sputter of small-arms' fire, punctuated by the occasional *whump-whump-whump* of 40-mm auto-cannon or the hammering of a machine-gun.

Returning to his command-post at the telecast station, the terrain-board showed that the perimeter of defense had been pushed out in a bulge at the north-

west corner; the TV-screen pictured a crude breast-
work of petrified tree-trunks, sandbags, mining
machinery, packing-cases and odds-and-ends, upon
which Wallingsby's native laborers were working under guard while a skirmish-line of Kragans had been
thrown out another four or five hundred yards and
were exchanging pot-shots with Skilkans on the gul-
lied hillside.

"Where's Colonel Quinton?" he asked. "She ought
to be taking a turn in the sack, now."

"She's taking one," Major Falkenberg, who had
commanded the action at the native-troops barracks
and the labor-camp, the night before, told him. "General Mordkovitz chased her off to bed a couple of
hours ago, called me in to take her place, and then
went out to replace me. Colonel Guilliford's in the
hospital; got hit about thirteen hundred. They're afraid
he's going to lose a leg."

"That's a bloody shame!" He pointed to the northwest corner of the perimeter on the screen. "Whose
idea was that?" he asked. "It's a good one; I ought
to have thought of it, myself."

"Your new adjutant," Falkenberg grinned. "She
asked somebody what those big domes, up there, were.
When they told her there were ten thousand tons of
thermoconcentrate, five thousand tons of blasting-ex-
plosives, and five tons of plutonium, under them, she
damned near fainted, and then she ordered that, right
away."

More reports came in. The entire garrison of the
small Residency at Kwurk, the most northern of the
eastern shore Free Cities, had arrived at Kankad's
Town in two hundred-foot contragravity scows and
five aircars. Two of the aircars arrived half an hour
behind the rest of the refugee flotilla, having turned

off at Keegark to pay their respects to King Orgzild. They reported the Keegark Residency in ruins, its central buildings vanished in a huge crater; the *Jan Smuts* and the *Christiaan De Wett* were still in the Company docks, both apparently damaged by the blast which had destroyed the Residency. One of the aircars had rocketed and machine-gunned some Keegarkans who appeared to be trying to repair them; the other blew up King Orgzild's nitroglycerine plant. Von Schlichten called Konkrook and ordered a bombing-mission against Keegark organized, to make sure the two ships stayed out of service.

The *Northern Star* was still bringing loyal troops into Krink. King Jonkvank, whom von Schlichten called, was highly elated.

"We are killing traitors wherever we find them!" he exulted. "The city is yellow with their blood; their heads are piled everywhere! How is it with you at Skilk?"

"We have killed many, also," von Schlichten boasted. "And tonight, we will kill more; we are preparing bombs of great destruction, which we will rain down upon Skilk until there is not one stone left upon another, or one infant of a day's age left alive!"

Jonkvank reacted as he was intended to. "Oh, no, general, don't do all that!" he exclaimed. "You promised me that I should have Skilk, on the word of a Terran. Are you going to give me a city of ruins and corpses? Ruins are no good to anybody, and I am not a Jeel, to eat corpses."

Von Schlichten shrugged. "When you are strong, you can flog your enemies with a whip; when you are weak, all you can do is kill them. If I had five thousand more troops, here . . ."

"Oh, I will send troops, as soon as I can," Jonkvank

hastened to promise. "All my best regiments: the Murderers, the Jeel-Feeders, the Corpse-Reapers, the Devastators, the Fear-Makers. But, now that we have stopped this sinful rebellion, here, I can't take chances that it will break out again as soon as I strip the city of troops."

Von Schlichten nodded. Jonkvank's argument made sense; he would have taken a similar position, himself.

"Well, get as many as you can over here, as soon as possible," he said. "We'll try to do as little damage to Skilk as we can, but..."

At 1830, Paula joined him for her breakfast, while he sat in front of the big screen, eating his dinner. There had been light ground-action along the southern end of the perimeter—King Firkked's regulars, reenforced by Zirk tribesmen and levies of townspeople, all of whom seemed to have firearms, were filtering in through the ruins of the labor-camp and the wreckage of the equipment-park—and there was renewed sniping from the mountainside. The long afternoon of the northern autumn dragged on; finally, at 2200, the sun set, and it was not fully dark for another hour. For some time, there was an ominous quiet, and then, at 0030, the enemy began attacking in force, driving herds of livestock—lumbering six-legged brutes bred by the North Ullerans for food—to test the defenses for electrified wire and land-mines. Most of these were shot down or blown up, but a few got as far as the wire, which, by now, had been strung and electrified completely around the perimeter.

Behind them came parties of Skilkan regulars with long-handled insulated cutters; a couple of cuts were made in the wire, and a section of it went dead. The line, at this point, had been rather thinly held; the defenders immediately called for air-support, and Jarman ordered fifteen of his remaining twenty airjeeps and five combat-cars into the fight. No sooner were they committed than the radar on the commercial airport control-tower picked up air vehicles approaching from the north, and the air-raid sirens began howling and the searchlights went on.

As a protection from the sudden fury of the summer and winter gales, the buildings were all low, thick-walled, and provided with steel doors and window-shutters which were electrically operated and centrally controlled. These slammed shut in every occupied building. The contragravity which had been sent to support the ground-defense at the south side of the Reservation turned to meet this new threat, and everything else available, including the four heavy airtanks, lifted up. Meanwhile, guns began firing from the ground and from rooftops.

There had been four aircars, ordinary passenger vehicles equipped with machine-guns on improvised mounts, and ten big lorries converted into bombers, in the attack. All the lorries, and all but one of the makeshift fighter-escort, were shot down, but not before explosive and thermoconcentrate bombs were dumped all over the place. One lorry emptied its load of thermoconcentrate-bombs on the control-building at the airport, starting a raging fire and putting the radar out of commission. A repair-shop at the ordnance-depot was set on fire, and a quantity of small-arms and machine-gun ammunition piled outside for transportation to the outer defenses blew up. An explosive bomb landed on the roof of the buiding between Company House and the telecast station, blowing a hole in the roof and demolishing the upper floor. And another load of thermoconcentrate, missing the power-plant, set fire to the dry grass between it and the ruins of the native-troops barracks.

Before the air-attack had been broken up, the soldiers of King Firkked and their irregular supporters were swarming through the dead section of wire. They had four or five big farm-tractors, nuclear-powered but unequipped with contragravity-generators, which they were using like ground-tanks of the First Century. This attack penetrated to the middle of the Reservation before it was stopped and the attackers either killed or driven out; for the first time since daybreak, the red-and-yellow lights came on around the power-plant.

As soon as the combined air and ground attack was beaten off, von Schlichten ordered all his available contragravity up, flying patrols around the Reservation and retaliatory bombing missions against Skilk, and began bombarding the city with his 90-mm guns. A number of fires broke out, and at about 0200 a huge expanding globe of orange-red flame soared up from the city.

"There goes Firkked's thermoconcentrate stock," he said to Paula, who was standing beside him in front of the screen.

Half an hour later, he discovered that he had been overly optimistic. Much of the enemy's supply of Terran thermoconcentrate had been destroyed, but enough remained to pelt the Reservation and the Company buildings with incendiaries, when a second and more severe air-attack developed, consisting of forty or fifty makeshift lorry-bombers and fifteen aircars. The previous attack von Schlichten had viewed in the screen at the telecast station; it was his questionable good fortune to observe the second one directly, having been out inspecting the defenses around the ordnance-depot at the time.

Like the first, the second air-attack was beaten off,

or, more exactly, down. Most of the enemy contra-gravity was destroyed; at least two dozen vehicles crashed inside the Reservation. As in the first instance, there was a simultaneous ground attack from the southern side, with a demonstration-attack at the north end. For a while, von Schlichten found himself fighting hand-to-hand, first with his pistol and then, when his ammunition was gone, with a picked-up rifle and bayonet. It was full daylight before the last of the attackers was either killed or driven out.

Five minutes later, while he was reloading his pistol-clips with salvaged cartridges, the *Northern Star* came bulking over the mountains from the west.

XI-

Of Princedoms Which Have Been Won by Conquest

Holstering his pistol, he raced for the telecast station, to receive a call from a Colonel Khalid ib'n Talal, a Zanzibar Arab, aboard the approaching ship.

"I've one of Jonkvank's regiments, the Jeel-Feeders, armed with Terran 9-mm rifles and a few bazookas; I have a company of our Zirks, with their mounts, and a battalion of the Sixth N.U.N.I.; I also have four 90-mm guns, Terran-manned," he reported. "What's the situation, general, and where do you want me to land?"

Von Schlichten described the situation succinctly, in an ancient and unprintable military cliche. "Try landing south of the Reservation, a little west of the ruins of the labor-camp," he advised. "The bulk of Firkked's army is in that section, and I want them run out as soon as possible. We'll give you all the contragravity and fire support we can."

The *Northern Star* let down slowly, firing her guns and dropping bombs; as she descended, rifle-fire spurted from all her lower-deck portholes. There was cheering, human and Ulleran, from inside the battered defense-perimeter; combat-cars, airjeeps, and improvised bombers lifted out to strafe the Skilkans on the ground, and the four airtanks moved out to take position and open fire with their 90-mm's, helping to

flush King Firkked's regulars and auxiliaries out of
the gullies and ruins and drive them south along the
mountain, away from where the ship would land and
also away from the city of Skilk. The *Northern Star*
set down quickly, and troops and artillery began to
be unloaded, joining in the fighting.

It was five hundred miles to Krink; three hours
after lifting out, the *Northern Star* was back again,
with two more of King Jonkvank's infantry regiments,
and by 1300, when the fourth load arrived from Krink,
the fighting was entirely on the eastern bank of the
dry Hoork River. This last contingent of reenforcements was landed in the eastern suburbs of Skilk and
began fighting their way into the city from the rear.

It was evident, however, that the pacification of
Skilk would not be accomplished as rapidly as von
Schlichten wished—street fighting, against a deter-
mined enemy, is notoriously slow work—and he decided to risk the *Northern Star* in an attack against
the Palace itself, and, over the objections of Paula
Quinton, Jules Keaveney, and Barney Mordkovitz, to
lead the attack in person.

Inside the city, he found that the Zirk cavalry from
Krink had thrust up one of the broader streets to within
a thousand yards of the Palace, and, supported by
infantry, contragravity, and a couple of airtanks, were
pounding and hacking at a mass of Skilkans whose
uniform lack of costume prevented distinguishing between soldiery and townsfolk. Very few of these, he
observed, seemed to be using firearms; with his glasses,
he could see them shooting with long northern air-
rifles and a few Takkad Sea crossbows. Either weapon
would shoot clear through a Terran or half-way through
an Ulleran at fifty yards, but at over two hundred they
were almost harmless. There were a few fires still

burning from the bombardment of the night before—
Ulleran, and particularly North Ulleran, cities did not
burn well—and the blaze which had consumed the
bulk of Firkked's stock of thermoconcentrate fuel had
long ago burned out, leaving an area of six or eight
blocks blackened and lifeless.

The ship let down, while the six combat-cars which
had accompanied her buzzed the Palace roof, strafing
it to keep it clear, and the Kragans aboard fired with
their rifles. She came to rest on seven-eights weight
reduction, and even before the gangplanks were run
out, the Kragans were dropping to the flat roof, running to stairhead penthouses and tossing grenades into
them.

The taking of the Palace was a gruesome business.
Knowing exactly how much mercy they would have
shown had they been storming the Residency, Firkked's
soldiers and courtiers fought desperately and had to
be exterminated, floor by floor, room by room, hallway by hallway. There was some attempt at escape
from the ground floor as von Schlichten and his Kragans fought their way down from above, but the
Northern Star and her escort of combat-cars and airjeeps bombed and machine-gunned and rocketed the
fugitives from above, and the loyal Zirk cavalry,
bursting through the mob, came up shooting and lancing. By this time, an aircar fitted with a sound-am-
plifier was circling overhead, while a loyal native-
officer of the Sixth N.U.N.I. shouted offers of quarter
and orders to the troops to spare any who surrendered.

Driving down from above, von Schlichten and his
Kragans slithered over floors increasingly greasy with
yellow Ulleran blood. He had picked up a broadsword
at the foot of the first stairway down; a little later, he
tossed it aside in favor of another, better balanced and

with a better guard. There was a furious battle at the doorways of the throne room; finally, climbing over the bodies of their own dead and the enemy's they were inside.

Here there was no question of quarter whatever, at least as long as Firkked lived; North Ulleran nobles did not surrender under the eyes of their king, and North Ulleran kings did not surrender their thrones alive. There was also a tradition, of which von Schlichten was mindful, that a king must only be killed by his conqueror, in personal combat, with steel.

With a wedge of Kragan bayonets around him and the picked-up broadsword in his hand, he fought his way to the throne, where Firkked waited, a sword in one of his upper hands, his Spear of State in the other, and a dagger in each lower hand. With his left hand, von Schlichten detached the bayonet from the rifle of one of his followers and went forward, trying not to think of the absurdity of a man of the Sixth Century A.E., the representative of a civilized Chartered Company, dueling to the death with swords with a barbarian king for a throne he had promised to another barbarian, or of what could happen on Uller if he allowed this four-armed monstrosity to kill him.

It was not as bad as it looked, however. The ornate Spear of State, in spite of its long, cruel-looking blade, was not an especially good combat-weapon, at least for one hand, and Firkked seemed confused by the very abundance of his armament. After a few slashes and jabs, von Schlichten knocked the unwieldy thing from his opponent's hand. This raised a fearful ululation from the Skilkan nobility, who had stopped fighting to watch the duel; evidently it was the very worse sort of a bad omen. Firkked, seemingly relieved

to be disencumbered of the thing, caught his sword
in both hands and aimed a roundhouse swing at von
Schlichten's head; von Schlichten dodged, crippled
one of Firkked's lower hands with a quick slash, and
lunged at the royal belly. Firkked used his remaining
dagger to parry, backed a step closer to his throne,
and took another swing with his sword, which von
Schlichten parried on the bayonet in his left hand.
Then, backing, he slashed at the inside of Firkked's
leg with the thousand-year-old *coup-de-Jarnac*.
Firkked, unable to support the weight of his dense-
tissued body on one leg, stumbled; von Schlichten ran
him neatly through the breast with his sword and
through the throat with the bayonet.

There was silence in the throne room for an instant,
and then, with a horrible collective shriek, the Skilkans threw down their weapons. One of von Schlichten's Kragans slung his rifle and picked up the Spear
of State with all four hands, taking his post ceremo-
niously behind the victor. A couple of others dragged
the body of Firkked to the edge of the dais, and one
of them drew his leaf-shaped short-sword and be-
headed it.

At mid-afternoon, von Schlichten was on the roof
of the Palace, holding the Spear of State, with Firkked's
head impaled on the point, while a Terran technician
aimed an audio-visual recorder.

"This," he said, with the geek-speaker in his mouth,
"is King Firkked's Spear of State, and here, upon it,
is King Firkked's head. Two days ago, Firkked was
at peace with the Company, and Firkked was King in
Skilk. If he had not dared raise his feeble hand against
the might of the Uller Company, he would still be

alive, and his Spear would still be borne behind him. So must all those who rise against the Company perish. . . . Cut."

The camera stopped. A Kragan came forward and took the Spear of State, with its grisly burden, carrying it to a nearby wall and leaning it up, like a piece of stage property no longer required for this scene but needed for the next. Von Schlichten took out his geek-speaker, wiped and pouched it, and took his cigarette case from his pocket.

"Well, this is the limit!" Paula Quinton, who had come up during the filming of the scene, exploded. "I thought you had to kill him yourself in order to encourage your soldiers; I didn't think you wanted to make a movie of it to show your friends. I'm through; you can find yourself a new adjutant!"

Von Schlichten tapped the cigarette on the gold-and-platinum case and stared at her through his monocle.

"You can't resign," he told her. "Resignations of officers are not being accepted until the end of hostilities. In any case, I shouldn't care to have you go; you're the best adjutant, Hideyoshi O'Leary not excepted, I ever had. Sit down, colonel." He lit the cigarette. "Your politico-military education still needs a little filling in.

"At Grank, we have two ships. One is the *Northern Lights,* sister ship of the *Northern Star.* The other is the cruiser *Procyon,* the only real warship on Uller, with a main battery of four 200-mm guns. How King Yoorkerk was able to get control of those ships I don't know, but there will be a board of inquiry and maybe a couple of courts-martial, when things get stabilized to a point where we can afford such luxuries. As it is, we need those ships desperately, and as soon as

he gets in, I'm sending Hideyoshi O'Leary to Grank
with the *Northern Star* and a load of Kragan Rifles,
to pry them loose. The audio-visual of which this is
the last scene is going to be one of the crowbars he's
going to use."

"Oh! I get it!" Her eyes widened with pleasure at
having finally caught on; she accepted the cigarette
and the light von Schlichten offered. "Good old *ner-
venkrieg!*"

"Yes. A little idea I adapted from my Nazi ancestors of four hundred and fifty years ago. Hideyoshi's
going to treat King Yoorkerk to a movie-show. Want
to bet he won't loosen up and release *Procyon* and
Northern Lights and unblockade the Grank Residency
after he sees that shot of Firkked's head leering at him
off the point of that overgrown asagai? As I said,
that's only the last scene, too. I've been having scenes
shot all through this fight; some of them are really
horrifying."

"But why did you have to fight Firkked yourself?"
she asked. "You took an awful chance, with two hands
to his four."

"Not so awful, remember what I told you about
the physical limitations of Ullerans. But I had to kill
him myself, with a sword; according to local custom
that makes me King of Skilk."

"Why, your Majesty!" She rose and curtsied mock-
ingly. "But I thought you were going to make Jonkvank King of Skilk."

He shook his head. "Just Viceroy," he corrected.
"I'm handing the Spear of State down to him, not up
to him; he'll reign as my vassal, and, consequently,
as vassal of the Company, and before long, he won't
be much more at Krink either. That'll take a little
longer—there'll have to be military missions, and

economic missions, and trade-agreements, and all the
rest of it, first—but he's on the way to becoming a
puppet-prince."

Half an hour later, a large and excessively ornate
air-launch, specially built at the Konkrook shipyards
for King Jonkvank, was sighted coming over the
mountain from the east. An escort of combat-cars was
sent to meet it, and a battalion of Kragans and the
survivors of Firkked's court were drawn up on the
Palace roof.

"His Majesty, Jonkvank, King of Krink!" the former herald of King Firkked's court, now herald to
King Carlos von Schlichten, shouted, banging on a
brass shield with the flat of his sword, as Jonkvank
descended from his launch, attended by a group of
his nobles and his Spear of State, with Hideyoshi
O'Leary and Francis X. Shapiro shepherding them.
As the guests advanced across the roof, the herald
banged again on his shield.

"His Majesty, Carlos von Schlichten,"—which
came out more or less as Karlok vonk Zlikdenk—
"King, by right of combat, of Skilk!"

Von Schlichten advanced to meet his fellow-mon-
arch, his own Spear of State, with Firkked's head still
grinning from it, two paces behind him.

Jonkvank stopped, his face contorted with saurian
rage.

"What is this?" he demanded. "You told me that
I could be King of Skilk; is this how a Terran keeps
his word?"

"A Terran's word is always good, Jonkvank," von
Schlichten replied, omitting the titles, as was proper
in one sovereign addressing another. "My word was
that you should reign in Skilk, and my word stands.
But these things must be done decently, according to

custom and law. I killed Firkked in single combat. Had I not done so, the Spear of Skilk would have been left lying, for any of the young of Firkked to pick up. Is that not the law?"

Jonkvank nodded grudgingly. "It is the law," he admitted.

"Good. Now, since I killed Firkked in lawful manner, his Spear is mine, and what is mine I can give as I please. I now give you the Spear of Skilk, to carry in my name, as I promised."

The Kragan who was carrying the ceremonial weapon tossed the head of Firkked from the point; another Kragan kicked it aside and advanced to wipe the spear-blade with a rag. Von Schlichten took the Spear and gave it to Jonkvank.

"This is not good!" one of the Skilkan nobles protested. He had a better right than any of the others to protest; he had, a few hours before, ridden in at the head of a company of his retainers to swear loyalty to the Company. "That you should rule over us, yes. You killed Firkked in single combat, and you are the soldier of the Company, which is mighty, as all here have seen. But that this foreigner be given the Spear of Skilk, that is not good!"

Some of the others, emboldened by his example, were jabbering agreement.

"Listen, all of you!" von Schlichten shouted. "Here is no question of Krink ruling over Skilk. Does it matter who holds the Spear of Skilk, when he does so in my name? And King Jonkvank will be no foreigner. He will come and live among you, and later he will travel back and forth between Krink and Skilk, and he will leave the Spear of Krink in Krink, and the Spear of Skilk in Skilk, and in Skilk he will be a Skilkan."

That seemed to satisfy everybody except Jonkvank, and he had wit enough not to make an issue of it. He even had the Spear of Krink carried back aboard his launch, out of sight, and when he accompanied von Schlichten, an hour later, to see Hideyoshi O'Leary off for Grank, he had the Spear of Skilk carried behind him. When he was alone with von Schlichten, in the room that had been King Firkked's bedchamber, however, he exploded: "What is all this foolishness which you promised these people in my name and which I must now carry out? That I am to leave the Spear of Skilk in Skilk and the Spear of Krink in Krink, and come here to live...."

"You wish to hold Skilk?" von Schlichten asked.

"I intend to hold Skilk. To begin with, there shall be a great killing here. A very great killing: of all those who advised that fool of a Firkked to start this business; of those who gave shelter to the false prophet, Rakkeed, when he was here; of the faithless priests who gave ear to his abominable heresies and allowed him to spew out his blasphemies in the temples; of those who sent spies to Krink, to corrupt and pervert my soldiers and nobles; of those who..."

"All that is as it should be," von Schlichten agreed. "Except that it must be done quickly and all at once, before the memories of these crimes fade from the minds of the people. And great care must be taken to kill only those who can be proven to be guilty of something; thus it will be said that the justice of King Jonkvank is terrible to evildoers but a protection and a shield to those who keep the peace and obey the laws. Thus you will gain the name of being a wise and just king. And when the priests are to be killed it should be done under the direction of those other priests who were faithful to the gods and whom King

Firkked drove out of their temples, and it must be done in the name of the gods. Thus will you be esteemed a pious, and not an impious, king. As to why you must be a Skilkan in Skilk, you heard the words of Flurknurk, and how the others agreed with him. It must not be allowed to seem that the city has come under foreign rule. And you must not change the laws, unless the people petition you to do so, nor must you increase the taxes, and you must not confiscate the estates of those who are put to death, for the death of parents is always forgiven before the loss of patrimonies. And you should select certain Skilkan nobles, and become the father of their young, and above all, you must leave none of the young of Firkked alive, to raise rebellion against you later."

Jonkvank nodded, deeply impressed. "By the gods, Karlok vonk Zlikdenk, this is wisdom! Now it is to be seen why the likes of Firkked cannot prevail against you, or against the Company as long as you are the Company's upper sword-arm!"

Honesty tempted von Schlichten, for a moment, to disclaim originality for the principles he had just enunciated, even at the price of trying to pronounce the name of Niccolo Machiavelli with a geek-speaker. On second thought, however, considerations of policy restrained him. If Jonkvank ever heard of *The Prince*, nothing would satisfy him short of an Ulleran translation, and von Schlichten would have been just about as happy over an Ulleran translation of a complete set of Bethe-cycle bomb specifications.

XII -

The Shadow of Niflheim

The sun slid lower and lower toward the horizon behind them as the aircar bulleted south along the broad valley and dry bed of the Hoork River, nearing the zone of equal day and night. Hassan Bogdanoff drove while Harry Quong finished his lunch, then changed places to begin his own. Von Schlichten got two bottles of beer from the refrigerated section of the lunch-hamper and opened one for Paula Quinton and one for himself.

"What are we going to do with these geeks,"—she was using the nasty and derogatory word unconsciously and by custom, now—"after this is all over? We can't just tell them, 'Jolly well played, nice game, wasn't it?' and go back to where we were Wednesday evening."

"No, we can't. There's going to have to be a Terran seizure of political power in every part of this planet that we occupy, and as soon as we're consolidated around and north of Takkad Sea, we're going to have to move in elsewhere," he replied. "Keegark, Konkrook, and the Free Cities, of course, will be relatively easy. They're in arms against us now, and we can take them over by force. We had to make that deal with Jonkvank, or, rather, I did, so that will be a slower process, but we'll get it done in time. If I know that pair as well as I think I do, Jonkvank and Yoorkerk will give us plenty of pretexts, before long. Then, we can start giving them government by law instead of by royal decree, and real courts of justice; put an end to the head-payment system, and to these arbitrary mass arrests and tax-delinquency imprisonments that are nothing but slave-raids by the geek princes on their own people. And, gradually, abolish serfdom. In a couple of centuries, this planet will be fit to admit to the Federation, like Odin and Freya."

"Well, won't that depend a lot on whom the Company sends here to take Harrington's place?"

"Unless I'm much mistaken, the Company will confirm me," he replied. "Administration on Uller is going to be a military matter for a long time to come, and even the Banking Cartel and the mercantile interests in the Company are going to realize that, and see the necessity for taking political control. The Federation Government owns a bigger interest in the Company than the public realizes, too; they've always favored it. And just to make sure, I'm sending Hid O'Leary to Terra on the next ship, to make a full report on the situation."

"You think it'll be cleared up by then? The *City of Montevideo* is due in from Niflheim in a little under three months."

"It'll have to be cleared up by then. We can't keep this war going more than a month, at the present rate. Police-action, and mopping-up, yes, full-scale war, no."

"Ammunition?" she asked.

He looked at her in pleased surprise. "Your education has been progressing, at that," he said. "You know, a lot of professional officers, even up to field rank in the combat branches, seem to think that ammo comes down miraculously from Heaven, in contra-

gravity lorries, every time they pray into a radio for
it. It doesn't; it has to be produced as fast as it's
expended, and we haven't been doing that. So we'll
have to lick these geeks before it runs out, because
we can't lick them with gunbutts and bayonets."

"Well, how about nuclear weapons?" Paula asked.
"I hate to suggest it—I know what they did on Mimir,
and Fenris, and Midgard, and what they did on Terra,
during the First Century. But it may be our only
chance."

He finished his beer and shoved the bottle into the
waste-receiver, then got out his cigarettes.

"I'd hate to have to make a decision like that,
Paula," he told her. "The military use of nuclear energy is the last—well, the next-to-last—thing I'd want
to see on Uller. Fortunately, or unfortunately, it's a
decision I won't have to make. There isn't a single
nuclear bomb on the planet. The Company's always
refused to allow them to be manufactured or stockpiled
here."

"I don't think there'd be any criticism of your making them, now, general. And there's certainly plenty
of plutonium. You could make A-bombs, at least."

"There isn't anybody here who even knows how
to make one. Most of our nuclear engineers could
work one up, in about three months, when we'd either
not need one or not be alive."

"Dr. Gomes, who came in on the *Pretoria*, two
weeks ago, can make them," she contradicted. "He
built at least a dozen of them on Niflheim, to use in
activating volcanoes and bringing ore-bearing lava to
the surface."

Von Schlichten's hand, bringing his lighter to the
tip of his cigarette, paused for a second. Then he

completed the operation, snapped it shut, and put it away.

"When did all this happen?"

She took time out for mental arithmetic; even a spaceship officer had to do that, when a question of interstellar time-relations arose.

"About three-fifty days ago, Galactic Standard. They'd put off the first shot, six bombs, before I got in from Terra. I saw the second shot a day or so before I left Niflheim on the *Canberra*. Dr. Gomes had to stay over till the *Pretoria* to put off the third shot. Why?"

"Did you run into a geek named Gorkrink, while you were on Nif?" he asked her. "And what sort of work was he doing?"

"Gorkrink? I don't seem to remember.... Oh, yes! He was helping Dr. Murillo, the seismologist. His year was up after the second shot; he came to Uller on the *Canberra*. Dr. Murillo was sorry to lose him. He understood Lingua Terra perfectly; Dr. Murillo could talk to him, the way you do with Kankad, without using a geek-speaker."

"Well, but what sort of work...?"

"Helping set and fire the A-bombs.... *Oh! Good Lord!*"

"You can say that again, and deal in Allah, Shiva, and Kali," von Schlichten told her. "Especially Kali.... Harry! See if you can get some more speed out of this can. I want to get to Konkrook while it's still there!"

It was full dark when Konkrook came in view beyond the East Konk Mountains, a lurid smear on the underside of the clouds, and, at Gongonk Island and at the Company farms to the south, a couple of bunches of searchlights fingering about in the sky. When von Schlichten turned on the outside sound-pickup, he could hear the distant tom-tomming of heavy guns, and the crash of shells and bombs. Keeping the car high enough to be above the trajectories of incoming shells, Harry Quong circled over the city while Hassan Bogdanoff talked to Gongkonk Island on the radio.

The city was in a bad way. There were seventy-five to a hundred big fires going, and a new one started in a rising ball of thermoconcentrate flame while they watched. The three gun-cutters, *Elmoran, Gaucho,* and *Bushranger,* and about fifty big freight lorries converted to bombers, were shuttling back and forth between the island and the city. The Royal Palace was on fire from end to end, and the entire waterfront and industrial district were in flames. Combat-cars and airjeeps were diving in to shell and rocket and machine-gun streets and buildings. He saw six big bomber-lorries move in dignified procession to unload, one after the other, on a row of buildings along what the Terrans called South Tenth Street, and on the roofs of buildings a block away, red and blue flares were burning, and he could see figures, both human and Ulleran, setting up mortars and machine-guns.

Landing on the top stage of Company House, on the island, they were met by a Terran whom von Schlichten had seen, a few days ago, bossing native-labor at the spaceport, but who was now wearing a major's insignia. He greeted von Schlichten with a salute which he must have learned from some movie about the ancient French Foreign Legion. Von Schlichten seriously returned it in kind.

"Everybody's down in the Governor-General's office, sir," he said. "Your office, that is. King Kankad's here with us, too."

He accompanied them to the elevator, then turned to a telephone; when von Schlichten and Paula reached the office, everybody was crowded at the door to greet them: Themistocles M'zangwe, his arm in a sling; Hans Meyerstein, the Johannesburg lawyer, who seemed to have even more Bantu blood than the brigadier-general; Morton Buhrmann, the Commercial Superintendent; Laviola, the Fiscal Secretary; a dozen or so other officers and civil administrators. There was a hubbub of greetings, and he was pleased to detect as much real warmth from the civil administration crowd as from the officers.

"Well, I'm glad to be back with you," he replied, generally. "And let me present Colonel Paula Quinton, my new adjutant; Hid O'Leary's on duty in the north. . . . Them, this was a perfectly splendid piece of work here; you can take this not only as a personal congratulation, but as a sort of unit citation for the whole crowd. You've all behaved simply above praise." He turned to King Kankad, who was wearing a pair of automatics in shoulder-holsters for his upper hands and another pair in cross-body belt holsters for his lower. "And what I've said for anybody else goes double for you, Kankad," he added, clapping the Kragan on the shoulder.

"All he did was save the lot of us!" M'zangwe said. "We were hanging on by our fingernails here till his people started coming in. And then, after you sent the *Aldebaran* . . ."

"Where is the *Aldebaran*, by the way? I didn't see her when I came in."

"Based on Kankad's, flying bombardment against

Keegark, and keeping an eye out for those ships.
Prinsloo caught the *De Wett* in the docks there and
smashed her, but the *Jan Smuts* got away, and we
haven't been able to locate the *Oom Paul Kruger*,
either. They're probably both on the Eastern Shore,
gathering up reenforcements for Orgzild," M'zangwe
said.

"Our ability to move troops rapidly is what's kept
us on top this long, and Orgzild's had plenty of time
to realize it," von Schlichten said. "When we get
Procyon down here, I'm going to send her out, with
a screen of light scout-vehicles, to find those ships
and get rid of them.... How's Hid been making out,
at Grank, by the way? I didn't have my car-radio on,
coming down."

That touched off another hubbub: "Haven't you
heard, general?"..."Oh, my God, this is simply out
of this continuum!"..."Well, tell him, somebody!"..."No, get Hid on the screen; it's his story!"

Somebody busied himself at the switchboard. The
rest of them sat down at the long conference-table.
Laviola and Meyerstein and Buhrmann were especially obsequious in seating von Schlichten in Sid
Harrington's old chair, and in getting a chair for Paula
Quinton. After a while, the jumbled colors on the big
screen resolved themselves into an image of Hideyoshi
O'Leary, grinning like a pussy-cat beside an empty
goldfish-bowl.

"Well, what happened?" von Schlichten asked, after
they had exchanged greetings. "How did Yoorkerk
like the movies? And did you get the *Procyon* and the
Northern Lights loose?"

"Yoorkerk was deeply impressed," O'Leary replied. "His story is that he is and always was the true
and ever-loving friend of the Company; he acted to

prevent quote certain disloyal elements unquote from harming the people and property of the Company. *Procyon's* on the way to Konkrook. I'm holding *Northern Lights* here and *Northern Star* at Skilk; where do you want them sent?"

"Leave *Northern Star* at Skilk, for the time being. Tell the Company's great and good friend King Yoorkerk that the Company expects him to contribute some soldiers for the campaign here and against Kee-gark, when that starts; be sure you get the best-armed and best-trained regiments he has, and get them down here as soon as possible. Don't send any of your Kragans or Karamessinis' troops here, though; hold them in Grank till we make sure of the quality of Yoorkerk's friendship."

"Well, general, I think we can be pretty sure, now. You see, he turned Rakkeed the Prophet over to me...."

"What?" Von Schlichten felt his monocle starting to slip and took a firmer grip on it. "Who?"

"Pay me, Them; he didn't drop it," Hideyoshi O'Leary said. "Why, Rakkeed the Prophet. Yoorkerk was holding our ships and our people in case we lost; he was also holding Rakkeed at the Palace in case we won. Of course, Rakkeed thought he was an honored guest, right up till Yoorkerk's guards dragged him in and turned him over to us...."

"That geek," von Schlichten said, "is too smart for his own good. Some of these days he's going to play both ends against the middle and both ends'll fold in on him and smash him." A suspicion occurred to him. "You sure this is Rakkeed? It would be just like Yoorkerk to try to sell us a ringer."

O'Leary shook his head solemnly. "I thought of that, right away. This is the real article; Karamessinis' Constabulary and Intelligence officers certified him for me. What do you want me to do, send him down to Konkrook?"

Von Schlichten shook his head. "Get the priests of the locally venerated gods to put him on trial for blasphemy, heresy, impersonating a prophet, practicing witchcraft without a license, or any other ecclesiastical crimes you or they can think of. Then, after he's been given a scrupulously fair trial, have the soldiers of King Yoorkerk behead him, and stick his head up over a big sign, in all native languages, 'Rakkeed the False Prophet.' And have audio-visuals made of the whole business, trial and execution, and be sure that the priests and Yoorkerk's officers are in the foreground and our people stay out of the pictures."

"Soap and towels, for General Pontius von Pilate!" Paula Quinton called out.

"That's an idea; I was wondering what to give Yoorkerk as a testimonial present," Hideyoshi O'Leary said. "A nice thirty-piece silver set!"

"Quite appropriate," von Schlichten approved. "Well, you did a first-class job. I want you back with us as soon as possible—incidentally, you're now a brigadier-general—but not till the situation Grank-Krink-Skilk is stabilized. And, eventually, you'll probably have to set up permanent headquarters in the north."

After Hideyoshi O'Leary had thanked him and signed off, and the screen was dark again, he turned to the others.

"Well, gentlemen, I don't think we need worry too much about the north, for the next few days. How long do you estimate this operation against Konkrook's going to take, to complete pacification, Them?"

"How complete is complete pacification, general?" Themistocles M'zangwe wanted to know. "If you mean to the end of organized resistance by larger than squad-size groups, I'd say three days, give or take twelve hours. Of course, there'll be small groups holding out for a couple of weeks, particularly in the farming country and back in the forest...."

"We can forget them; that's minor-tactics stuff. We'll need to keep some kind of an occupation force here for some time; they can deal with that. We'll have to get to work on Keegark, as soon as possible; after we've reduced Keegark, we'll be able to reorganize for a campaign against the Free Cities on the Eastern Shore."

"Begging your pardon, general, but reduce is a mild word for what we ought to do to Keegark," Hans Meyerstein said. "We ought to raze that city as flat as a football field, and then play football on it with King Orgzild's head."

"Any special reason?" von Schlichten asked. "In addition to the Blount-Lemoyne massacre, that is?"

"I should say so, general!" Themistocles M'zangwe backed Meyerstein up. "Bob, you tell him."

Colonel Robert Grinell, the Intelligence officer, got up and took the cigar out of his mouth. He was short and round-bodied and bald-headed, but he was old Terran Federation Regular Army.

"Well, general, we've been finding out quite a bit about the genesis of this business, lately," he said. "From up north, it probably looked like an all-Rakkeed show; that's how it was supposed to look. But the whole thing was hatched at Keegark, by King Orgzild. We've managed to capture a few prominent Konkrookans"—he named half a dozen—"who've been made to talk, and a number of others have come in voluntarily and furnished information. Orgzild conceived the scheme in the beginning; Rakkeed was just the messenger-boy. My face gets the color of the Company trademark every time I think that the whole thing was planned for over a year, right under our noses, even to the signal that was to touch the whole thing off...."

"The poisoning of Sid Harrington, and our announcement of his death?" von Schlichten asked.

"You figured that out yourself, sir? Well, that was it." Grinell went on to elaborate, while von Schlichten tried to keep the impatience out of his face. Beside him, Paula Quinton was fidgeting, too; she was thinking, as he was, of what King Orgzild and Prince Gorkrink were doing now. "And I know positively that the order for the poisoning of Sid Harrington came from the Keegarkan Embassy here, and was passed down through Gurgurk and Keeluk to this geek here who actually put the poison in the whiskey."

"Yes. I agree that Keegark should be wiped out, and I'd like to have an immediate estimate on the time it'll take to build a nuclear bomb to do the job. One of the old-fashioned plutonium fission A-bombs will do quite well."

Everybody turned quickly. There was a momentary silence, and then Colonel Evan Colbert, of the Fourth Kragan Rifles, the senior officer under Themistocles M'zangwe, found his voice.

"If that's an order, general, we'll get it done. But I'd like to remind you, first, of the Company policy on nuclear weapons on this planet."

"I'm aware of that policy. I'm also aware of the reason for it. We've been compelled, because of the lack of natural fuel on Uller, to set up nuclear power reactors and furnish large quantities of plutonium to the geeks to fuel them. The Company doesn't want the natives here learning of the possibility of using nuclear energy for destructive purposes. Well, gentlemen, that's a dead issue. They've learned it, thanks to our people on Niflheim, and unless my estimate is entirely wrong, King Orgzild already has at least one First-Century Nagasaki-type plutonium bomb. I am inclined to believe that he had at least one such bomb, probably more, at the time when orders were sent to his embassy here, for the poisoning of Governor-General Harrington."

With that, he selected a cigarette from his case, offered it to Paula, and snapped his lighter. She had hers lit, and he was puffing on his own, when the others finally realized what he had told them.

"That's impossible!" somebody down the table shouted, as though that would make it so. Another—one of the civil administration crowd—almost exactly repeated Jules Keaveney's words at Skilk: "What the hell was Intelligence doing, sleeping?"

"General von Schlichten," Colonel Grinell took oblique cognizance of the question, "you've just made, by implication, a most grave charge against my department. If you're not mistaken in what you've just said, I deserve to be court-martialed."

"I couldn't bring charges against you, colonel; if it were a court-martial matter, I'd belong in the dock with you," von Schlichten told him. "It seems, though, that a piece of vital information was possessed by those who were unable to evaluate it, and until this afternoon, I was ignorant of its existence. Colonel Quinton, suppose you repeat what you told me, on the way down from Skilk."

"Well, general, don't you think we ought to have Dr. Gomes do that?" Paula asked. "After all, he constructed those bombs on Niflheim, and it'll be he who'll have to build ours."

"That's right." He looked around. "Where's Dr. Lourenco Gomes, the nuclear engineer who came in on the *Pretoria*, two weeks ago? Send out for him, and get him in here at once."

There was another awkward silence. Then Kent Pickering, the chief of the Gongonk Island power-plant, cleared his throat.

"Why, general, didn't you know? Dr. Gomes is dead. He was killed during the first half hour of the uprising."

XIII-

A Bag of Tricks
We Don't Have

He flinched inwardly, and tightened his eye-muscles on the edge of the monocle to keep from flinching physically as well, trying to freeze out of his face the consternation he felt.

"That's bad, Kent," he said. "Very bad. I'd been counting heavily on Dr. Gomes to design a bomb of our own."

"Well, general, if you please." That was Air-Commodore Leslie Hargreaves. "You say you suspect that King Orgzild has developed a nuclear bomb. If that's true, it's a horrible danger to all of us. But I find it hard to believe that the Keegarkans could have done so, with their resources and at their technological level. Now, if it had been the Kragans, that would have been different, but..."

"Paula, you'd better carry on and explain what you told me, and add anything else you can think of that might be relevant.... Is that sound-recorder turned on? Then turn it on, somebody; we want this taped."

Paula rose and began talking: "I suppose you all understand what conditions are on Niflheim, and how these Ulleran native workers are employed; however, I'd better begin by explaining the purpose for which these nuclear bombs were designed and used...."

He smiled; she realized that he needed time to think, and she was stalling to provide it. He drew a

pencil and pad toward him and began doodling in a
bored manner, deliberately closing his mind to what
she was saying. There were two assumptions, he considered: first, that King Orgzild already possessed a
nuclear bomb which he could use when he chose, and,
second, that in the absence of Dr. Gomes, such a
bomb could only be produced on Gongonk Island after
lengthy experimental work. If both of these assumptions were true, he had just heard the death-sentence
of every Terran on Uller. The first he did not for a
moment doubt. The reasons for making it were too
good. He dismissed it from further consideration and
concentrated on the second.

". . . what's known as a Nagasaki-type bomb, the
first type of plutonium-bomb developed," Paula was
saying. "Really, it's a technological antique, but it
was good enough for the purpose, and Dr. Gomes
could build it with locally available materials. . . ."

That was the crux of it. The plutonium bomb, from
a military standpoint, was as obsolete as the flintlock
musket had been at the time of the Second World
War. He reviewed, quickly, the history of weapons-
development since the beginning of the Atomic Era.
The emphasis, since the end of the Second World
War, had all been on nuclear weapons and rocket-
missiles. There had been the H-bomb, itself obsoles-
cent, and the Bethe-cyle bomb, and the subneutron
bomb, and the omega-ray bomb, and the nega-matter
bomb, and then the end of civilization in the Northern
Hemisphere and the rise of the new civilization in
South America and South Africa and Australia. Today, the small-arms and artillery his troops were using
were merely slight refinements on the weapons of the
First Century, and all the modern nuclear weapons
used by the Terran Federation were produced at the

Space Navy base on Mars, by a small force of experts whose skills were almost as closed to the general scientific and technical world as the secrets of a medieval guild. The old A-bomb was an historical curiosity, and there was nobody on Uller who had more than a layman's knowledge of the intricate technology of modern nuclear weapons. There were plenty of good nuclear-power engineers on Gongonk Island, but how long would it take them to design and build a plutonium bomb?

". . . also has a good understanding of Lingua Terra," Paula was saying. "He and Dr. Murillo conversed bilingually, just as I've heard General von Schlichten and King Kankad talking to one another. I haven't any idea whether or not Gorkrink could read Lingua Terra, or, if so; what papers or plans he might have seen."

"Just a minute, Paula," he said. "Colonel Grinell, what does your branch have on this Gorkrink?"

"He's the son of King Orgzild, and the daughter of Prince Jurnkonk," Grinell said. "We knew he'd signed on for Nif, two years ago, but the story we got was that he'd fallen out of favor at court and had been exiled. I can see, now, that that was planted to mislead us. As to whether or not he çan read Lingua Terra, my belief is that he can. We know that he can understand it when spoken. He could have learned to read at one of those schools Mohammed Ferriera set up, ten or fifteen years ago."

"And Dr. Gomes and Dr. Murillo and Dr. Livesey left papers and plans lying around all over the place," Paula added. "If he went to Niflheim as a spy, he could have copied almost anything."

"Well, there you have it," von Schlichten said. "When Gorkrink found out that plutonium can be used for bombs, he began gathering all the information he could. And as soon as he got home, he turned it all over to Pappy Orgzild."

"That still doesn't mean that the Kee-geeks were able to do anything with it," Air-Commodore Hargreaves argued.

"I think it does," von Schlichten differed. "As soon as Orgzild would hear about the possibility of making a plutonium bomb, he'd set up an A-bomb project, and don't think of it in terms of the old First Century Manhattan Project. There would be no problem of producing fissionables—we've been scattering refined plutonium over this planet like confetti."

"Well, an A-bomb's a pretty complicated piece of mechanism, even if you have the plans for it," Kent Pickering said. "As I recall, there have to be several subcritical masses of plutonium, or U-235, or whatever, blown together by shaped charges of explosive, all of which have to be fired simultaneously. That would mean a lot of electrical fittings that I can't see these geeks making by hand."

"I can," Paula said. "Have you ever seen the work these native jewelers do? And didn't you tell me about a clockwork thing they have at the university here, to show the apparent movements of the sun...."

"That's right," von Schlichten said. "And what they couldn't make, they could have bought from us; we've sold them a lot of electrical equipment."

"All right, they could have built an A-bomb," Buhrmann said. "But did they?"

"We assume they tried to. Gorkrink got back from Nif on the *Canberra,* three months ago," von Schlichten said. "If Orgzild decided to build an A-bomb, he wouldn't give the signal for this uprising until he either had one or knew he couldn't make one, and he

wouldn't give up trying in only three months. There-
fore, I think we can assume that he succeeded, and
had succeeded at the time he sent Gorkrink here to
get that four tons of plutonium we let him have, and,
incidentally, to tell Ghroghrank to pass the word to
have Sid Harrington poisoned according to plan."

"Then why didn't he just use it on us at the start
of the uprising?" Meyerstein wanted to know.

"Why should he? Getting rid of us is only the first
step in Orgzild's plan," Grinell said. "Back as far as
geek history goes, the Kings of Keegark have been
trying to conquer Konkrook and the Free Cities and
make themselves masters of the whole Takkad Sea
area. Let Konkrook wipe us out, and then he can move
in his troops and take Konkrook. Or, if we beat off
the geeks here, as we seem to be doing, he can bomb
us out and then move in on Konkrook. I think that as
long as we're fighting here, he'll wait. The more
damage we do to Konkrook, the easier it'll be for
him."

"Then we'd better start dragging our feet on the
Konkrook front," Laviola said. "And get busy trying
to build a bomb of our own."

Von Schlichten looked up at the big screen, on
which the battle of Konkrook was being projected
from an overhead pickup.

"I'll agree on the second half of it," von Schlichten
said. "And we'll also have to set up some kind of
security-patrol system against bombers from Keegark.
And as soon as *Procyon* gets here, we'll have to send
her out to hunt down and destroy those two Boer-
class freighters, the *Jan Smuts* and the *Kruger*. And
we'll have to arrange for protection of Kankad's Town;
that's sure to be another of Orgzild's high-priority
targets. As to the action against Konkrook, I'll rely

on your advice, Them. Can we delay the fall of the city for any length of time?"

M'zangwe shook his head. "When we divert contragravity to security-patrol work, the ground action'll slow up a little, of course. But the geeks are about knocked out, now."

"The hell with it, then. I doubt if we'd be able to buy much time from Orgzild by delaying victory in the city, and we'll probably need the troops as workers over here." He turned to Pickering. "Dr. Pickering, what sort of a crew can you scrape together to design a bomb for us?" he asked.

"Well, there's Martirano, and Sternberg, and Howard Fu-Chung, and Piet van Reenen, and..." He nodded to himself. "I can get six or eight of them in here in about twenty minutes; I'll have a project set up and working in a couple of hours. There has to be somebody qualified on duty at the plant, all the time, of course, but..."

"All right, call them in. I want the bomb finished by yesterday afternoon. And everybody with you, and you, yourself, had better revert to civilian status. This isn't something you can do by the numbers, and I don't want anybody who doesn't know what it's all about pulling rank on your outfit. Go ahead, call in your gang, and let me know what you'll be able to do, as soon as possible."

He turned to Hargreaves. "Les, you'll have charge of flying the security patrols, and doing anything else you can to keep Orgzild from bombing us before we can bomb him. You'll have priority on everything second only to Pickering."

Hargreaves nodded. "As you say, general, we'll have to protect Kankad's, as well as this place. It's about five hundred miles from here to Kankad's, and eight-fifty miles from Kankad's to Keegark...."

He stopped talking to von Schlichten, and began muttering to himself, running over the names of ships, and the speeds and pay-load capacities of airboats, and distances. In about five minutes, he would have a programme worked out; in the meantime, von Schlichten could only be patient and contain himself. He looked along the table, and caught sight of a thin-faced, saturnine-looking man in a green shirt, with a colonel's three concentric circles marked on the shoulders in silver-paint. Emmett Pearson, the communications chief.

"Emmett," he said, "those orbiters you have strung around this planet, two thousand miles out, for telecast rebroadcast stations. How much of a crew could be put on one of them?"

Pearson laughed. "Crew of what, general? White mice, or trained cockroaches? There isn't room inside one of those things for anything bigger to move around."

"Well, I know they're automatic, but how do you service them?"

"From the outside. They're only ten feet through, by about twenty in length, with a fifteen-foot ball at either end, and everything's in sections, which can be taken out. Our maintenance-gang goes up in a thing like a small spaceship, and either works on the outside in spacesuits, or puts in a new section and brings the unserviceable one down here to the shops."

"Ah, and what sort of a thing is this small spaceship, now?"

"A thing like a pair of fifty-ton lorries, with airlocks between, and connected at the middle; airtight, of course, and pressurized and insulated like a spaceship. One side's living quarters for a six-man crew—some-

times the gang's out for as long as a week at a time—
and the other side's a workshop."

That sounded interesting. With contragravity, of
course, terms like "escape-velocity" and "mass-ratio"
were of purely antiquarian interest.

"How long," he asked Pearson, "would it take to
fit that vehicle with a full set of detection instruments—radar, infrared and ultraviolet vision, elec-
tron-telescope, heat and radiation detectors, the whole
works—and spot it about a hundred to a hundred and
fifty miles above Keegark?"

"That I couldn't say, general," Emmett Pearson
replied. "It'd have to be a shipyard job, and a lot of
that stuff's clear outside my department. Ask Air-
Commodore Hargreaves."

"Les!" he called out. "Wake up, Les!"

"Just a second, general." Hargreaves scribbled
frantically on his pad. "Now," he said, raising his
head. "What is it, sir?"

"Emmett, here, has a junior-grade spaceship that
he uses to service those orbital telecast-relay stations
of his. He'll tell you what it's like. I want it fitted
with every sort of detection device that can be crammed
into or onto it, and spotted above Keegark. It should,
of course, be high enough to cover not only the Keegark area, but Konkrook, Kankad's, and the lower
Hoork and Konk river-valleys."

"Yes, I get it." Hargreaves snatched up a phone,
punched out a combination, and began talking rapidly
into it in a low voice. After a while, he hung up. "All
right, Mr. Pearson—Colonel Pearson, I mean. Have
your space-buggy sent around to the shipyard. My
boys'll fix it up." He made a note on another piece
of paper. "If we live through this, I'm going to have
a couple of supra-atmosphere ships in service on this

planet.... Now, general, I have a tentative setup. We're
going to need the *Elmoran* for patrol work south and
east of Konkrook, and the *Gaucho* and *Bushranger*
to the north and northeast, based on Konkad's. We'll
keep the *Aldebaran* at Kankad's, and use her for emer-
gencies. And we'll have patrols of light contragravity
like this." He handed a map, with red-pencil and blue-
pencil markings, along to von Schlichten. "Red are
Kankad-based; blue are Konkrook-based."

"That looks all right," von Schlichten said. "There's
another thing, though. We want scout-vehicles to cover
the Keegark area with radiation-detectors. These geeks
are quite well aware of radiation-danger from fissionables, but they're accustomed to the ordinary indus-
trial-power reactors, which are either very lightly
shielded or unshielded on top. We want to find out
where Orgzild's bomb-plant is."

"Yes, general, as soon as we can get radiation
detectors sent out to Kankad's, we'll have a couple
of fast aircars fitted with them for that job."

"We have detectors, at our laboratory and reaction-
plant," Kankad said. "And my people can make more,
as soon as you want them." He thought for a moment.
"Perhaps I should go to the town, now. I could be of
more use there than here."

Kent Pickering, who had been talking with his experts at a table apart, returned.

"We've set up a programme, general," he said.
"It's going to be a lot harder than I'd anticipated.
None of us seem to know exactly what we have to
do in building one of those things. You see, the uranium or plutonium fission-bomb's been obsolete for
over four hundred years. It was a classified-secret
matter long after its obsolescence, because it hadn't
been rendered any the less deadly by being

superseded—there was that A-bomb that the Christian
Anarchist Party put together at Buenos Aires in 378
A.E., for instance. And then, after it was declassified,
it had been so far superseded that it was of only antiquarian interest; the textbooks dealt with it only in
general terms. The principles, of course, are part of
basic nuclear science; the "secret of the A-bomb" was
just a bag of engineering tricks that we don't have,
and which we will have to rediscover. Design of tampers, design of the chemical-explosive charges to bring
subcritical masses together, case-design, detonating
mechanism, things like that.

"The complete data on even the old Hiroshima and
Nagasaki types is still in existence, of course. You
can get it at places like the University of Montevideo
Library, or Jan Smuts Memorial Library at Cape Town.
But we don't have it here. We're detailing a couple
of junior technicians to make a search of the library
here on Gongonk Island, but we're not optimistic. We
just can't afford to pass up any chance, even when it
approaches zero-probability."

Von Schlichten nodded. "That's about what I'd
expected," he said. "I suppose Gomes got his data out
of one of the dustier storage-stacks at Jan Smuts or
Montevideo, in the first place.... Well, I still want
that bomb finished by yesterday afternoon, but since
that's impractical, you'll have to take a little—but as
little as possible—longer."

"What are we going to do about publicity on this?"
Howlett, the personnel man, asked. "We don't want
this getting out in garbled form—though how it could
be made worse by garbling I couldn't guess—and
having the troops watching the sky over their shoulders and going into a panic as soon as they saw something they didn't understand."

"No, we don't. I've seen a couple of troop-panics," von Schlichten said. "There can't be anything much worse than a panic."

"I think the Terrans ought to be told the worst," Hargreaves said. "And told that our only hope is to get a bomb of our own built and dropped first. As to the Kragans... What do you think, King Kankad?"

"Tell them that we are building a bomb to destroy Keegark; that we are running short of ammunition, and that it is our only hope of finishing the war before the ammunition is gone," Kankad said. "Tell them something of what sort of a bomb it is. But do not tell them that King Orgzild already has such a bomb. Old Kankad, who made me out of himself, told me about how our people fled in panic from the weapons of the Terrans, when your people and mine were still enemies. This thing is to the weapons they faced then as those weapons were to the old Kragans' spears and bows.... And when the geeks from Grank come here, tell them that we are winning and that if they fight well, they can share the loot of Konkrook and Keegark."

Von Schlichten looked up at the big screen. Already, Themistocles M'zangwe had ordered the Channel Battery to reduce fire; the big guns were firing singly, in thirty-second-interval salvos. There was less bombing, too; contragravity was being drawn out of the battle.

"Well, we all have things to do," he said, "and I think we've discussed everything there is to discuss. Anybody think of anything we've forgotten?... Then we're adjourned."

He and Paula Quinton took the elevator to the roof, and sat side by side, silently watching the conflagration that was raging across the channel and the nearer flashes of the big guns along the island's city side.

"Wednesday night, I thought we were all cooked," Paula told him. "Cleaning up the north in two days seemed like an impossibility, too. Maybe you'll do it again."

"If I pull this one out of the fire, I won't be a general; I'll be a magician," he said. "Pickering'll be a magician, I mean; he's the boy who'll save our bacon, if it's saveable." He looked somberly across the flame-reflecting water. "Let's not kid ourselves; we're just kicking and biting at the guards on the way up the gallows-steps."

"Well, why stop till the trap's sprung?" she asked. "What'll happen to these people on this planet, after we're atomized?"

"That I don't want to think about. Kankad's Town will get the second bomb; Orgzild won't dare leave the Kragans after he's wiped us out. Yoorkerk and Jonkvank, in the north, will turn on Keaveney and Shapiro and Karamessinis and Hid O'Leary and wipe them out. And when the next ship gets in here and they find out what happened, they'll send the Federation Space Navy, and this planet'll get it worse than Fenris did. They'll blast anything that has four arms and a face like a lizard. . . ."

Half a dozen aircars lifted suddenly from the airport and streaked away to the northeast. As they went past, in the light of the burning city, he could see that at least three of them had multiple rocket-launchers on top. In a matter of seconds, a gun-cutter raced after them, and a second, which had been over Konkrook, jettisoned a bomb and turned away to follow.

"Maybe that's it," Paula said.

"Well, if it is, we won't be any better off anywhere else than here," he told her. "Let's stay and watch."

After what seemed like a long time, however, a twinkle of lights showed over the East Konk Mountains. They weren't the flashes of explosions; some were magnesium flares, and some were the lights of a ship.

"That's *Procyon,* from Grank," he said. "Everybody gets a good mark for this—detection stations, interceptors, gun-cutters. If that had been it, there'd have been a good chance of stopping it." He felt better than he had since Pickering had told him that Lourenço Gomes was dead. "It's a good thing Gorkrink didn't pick up any dope on guided missiles, while he was at it. As long as they have to deliver it with contragravity, we have a chance."

They rose from the balustrade where they had been sitting, and, for the first time, he discovered that he had had his left arm over her shoulder and that she had had her right hand resting on the point of his right hip, just above his pistol. He picked up the folder of papers she had been carrying, and put her into the elevator ahead of him, and it was only when they parted on the living-quarters level that he recalled having followed the older protocol of gallantry rather than the precedence of military rank.

XIV -

The Reviewers
Panned Hell Out of It

He woke with a guilty start and looked up at the clock on the ceiling; it was 0945. Kicking himself free of the covers, he slid his feet to the floor and sprinted for the bathroom. While he was fussing to get the shower adjusted to the right temperature, he bludgeoned his conscience by telling himself that a wide-awake general is more good than a half-asleep general, that there was nothing he could do but hope that Hargreaves's patrols would keep the bomb away from Konkrook until Pickering's brain-trust came up with one of their own, and that the fact that the commander-in-chief was making sack-time would be much better for morale than the spectacle of him running around in circles. He shaved carefully; a stubble of beard on his chin might betray the fact that he was worried. Then he dressed, put his monocle in his eye, and called the headquarters that had been set up in Sid Harrington's—now his—office. A girl at the switchboard appeared on his screen, and gave place to Paula Quinton, who had been up for the past two hours.

"The *Northern Lights* got in about three hours ago, general," she told him. "She had four of King Yoorkerk's infantry regiments aboard—the Seventh, Glorious-and-Terrible, the Fourth, Firm-in-Adversity, the Second, Strength-of-the-Throne, and the Twelfth, Forever-Admirable. They're the sorriest-looking rab-

ble I ever saw, but Hideyoshi says they're the best
Yoorkerk has, and they all have Terran-style rifles.
General M'zangwe broke them into battalions, and
put a battalion in with each of the Kragan regiments.
I think they're more afraid of the Kragans than they
are of the rebels."

He nodded. That was probably the best way to
employ them, within the existing situation. The trouble was, Them M'zangwe was incurably tactical-
minded. Put those geeks of Yoorkerk's in with the
Kragans and they'd be most useful in conquering
Konkrook, but the trouble was that, after associating
with Kragans, they might develop into reasonably good
troops themselves, to the undesired improvement of
King Yoorkerk's army. On the other hand maybe not.
Keep them in Company service long enough, and they
might want to forget about Yoorkerk and stay there.

"How's the situation over in town?" he asked.

"Well, it's slowing up, since we began pulling
contragravity out," she told him, "but the geeks are
breaking up rapidly.... Oh, there was something funny
about that hassle, last evening, when the *Procyon*
came in. Two contragravity vehicles, an aircar and
an air-lorry, that went out to meet the ship, are un-
accounted for."

"You mean two of our vehicles are missing?"

She shook her head, frowning in perplexity. "Well,
no. All the vehicles that answered that unidentified-
aircraft alert returned, but there were these two that
went out that we haven't any record of. Colonel Grinell is investigating, but he can't find out anything...."

"Tell him not to waste any more time," he said.
"Those two were probably geeks from Konkrook. You
know, that's how the von Schlichten family got out

of Germany, in the Year Three—flew a bomber to Spain. The Konkrook war-criminals are getting out before the Army of Occupation moves in."

"Well, the posts at the old Kragan castles report some contragravity, and parties riding 'saurs, moving west from the city," she told him. "There are a lot of refugees on the roads. And combat reports from Konkrook agree that resistance is getting weaker every hour. . . . And the supra-atmosphere observation-craft—they're beginning to call her the *Sky-Spy*—is up a hundred and fifty miles over Keegark. We have radar and vision screens and telemetered radiation and other detectors here, tuned to her. They're installing a similar set on the *Northern Lights* at the shipyard. By the way, Air-Commodore Hargreaves wants to know if he can take a pair of 155-mm rifles from the Channel Battery and mount them on the *Lights*."

"Yes, of course, he can have anything he wants, as long as it isn't urgently needed for the bomb project."

"*Sky-Spy* reports normal contragravity traffic between Keegark and the farming-villages around—air-cars, lorries, a few scows—but nothing suspicious. No trace of either of the Boer-class ships. Kankad's people are building receiving sets to install on the *Procyon* and the *Aldebaran,* and another set for Kankad's Town. Pickering and his people are still working, but they all look pretty frustrated. They have Major Thornton, at the ammunition plant, doing experimental work on chemical-explosive charges to bring the subcritical masses together and hold them together till an explosion can be produced; they're using most of the skilled electrical and electronics people to work up a detonating device. That's why Kankad's people are doing most of the detection-device work. Hargreaves is fitting a lot of small craft—

combat-cars and civilian aircars—with radar sets, to use for patrolling."

"That sounds good," von Schlichten said. "I'll be around and see how things are, after I've had some breakfast."

He had breakfast at the main cafeteria, four floors down; there wasn't as much laughing and talking as usual, but the crowd there seemed in good spirits. He spent some time at headquarters, watching Keegark by TV and radar. So far, nothing had been done about direct reconnaissance over Keegark with radiation-detectors, but Hargreaves reported that a couple of privately owned aircars were being fitted for the job.

He made a flying inspection trip around the island, and visited the farms south of the city, on the mainland, and, finally, made a sweep in the command-car over the city itself. Reconnaissance in person was an archaic and unprogressive procedure, and it was a good way to get generals killed, but one could see a lot of things that would be missed on TV. He let down several times in areas that had already been taken, and talked to company and platoon officers. For one thing, King Yoorkerk's flamboyantly named regiments weren't quite as bad as Paula had thought. She'd been spoiled by the Kragans in her appreciation of other native troops. They had good, standard-quality, Volund-made arms; they were brave and capable; and they had been just enough insulted by being integrated into Kragan regiments to try to make a good showing.

By noon, resistance in the city was beginning to cave in. Surrender flags were appearing on one after another of the Konkrookan rebel strong-points, and at 1430, after he had returned to the Island, a delegation, headed by the Konkrookan equivalent of Lord

Mayor and composed largely of prominent merchants, came across the channel under a flag of truce to surrender the city's Spear of State, with abject apologies for not having Gurgurk's head on the point of it. Gurgurk, they reported, had fled to Keegark by air the night before, which explained the incident of the unaccountable aircar and lorry. The Channel Battery stopped firing, and, with the exception of an occasional spatter of small-arms fire, the city fell silent.

At 1600, von Schlichten visited the headquarters Pickering had set up in the office building at the power-plant. As he stepped off the lift on the third floor, a girl, running down the hall with her arms full of papers in folders, collided with him; the load of papers flew in all directions. He stooped to help her pick them up.

"Oh, general! Isn't it wonderful?" she cried. "I just can't believe it!"

"Isn't what wonderful?" he asked.

"Oh, don't you know? They've got it!"

"Huh? They have?" He gathered up the last of the big envelopes and gave them to her. "When?"

"Just half an hour ago. And to think, those books were around here all the time, and . . . Oh, I've got to run!" She disappeared into the lift.

Inside the office, one of Pickering's engineers was sitting on the middle of his spinal column, a stenograph-phone in one hand and a book in the other. Once in a while, he would say something into the mouthpiece of the phone. Two other nuclear engineers had similar books spread out on a desk in front of them; they were making notes and looking up references in the *Nuclear Engineers' Handbook*, and making calculations with their sliderules. There was a huddle around the drafting-boards, where two more such books were in use.

"Well, what's happened?" he demanded, catching Pickering by the arm as he rushed from one group to another.

"Ha! We have it!" Pickering cried. "Everything we need! Look!"

He had another of the books under his arm. He held it out to von Schlichten, and von Schlichten suddenly felt sicker than he had ever felt since, at the age of fourteen, he had gotten drunk for the first time. He had seen men crack up under intolerable strain before, but this was the first time he had seen a whole roomful of men blow their tops in the same manner.

The book was a novel—a jumbo-size historical novel, of some seven or eight hundred pages. Its dust-jacket bore a slightly-more-than-bust-length picture of a young lady with crimson hair and green eyes and jade earrings and a plunging—not to say power-diving—neckline that left her affiliation with the class of Mammalia in no doubt whatever. In the background, a mushroom-topped smoke-column rose, and away from it something intended to be a four-motor propeller-driven bomber of the First Century was racing madly. The title, he saw, was *Dire Dawn*, and the author was one Hildegarde Hernandez.

"Well, it has a picture of an A-bomb explosion on it," he agreed.

"It has more than that; it has the whole business. Case specifications, tampers, charge design, detonating device, everything. Why, the end-papers even have diagrams, copies of the original Nagasaki-bomb drawings. Look."

Von Schlichten looked. He had no more than the

average intelligent layman's knowledge of nuclear physics—enough to recharge or repair a conversion-unit—but the drawings looked authentic enough. They seemed to be copies of ancient blueprints, lettered in First Century English, with Lingua Terra translations added, and marked TOP SECRET and U.S. ARMY CORPS OF ENGINEERS and MANHATTAN EN-GINEERING DISTRICT.

"And look at this!" Pickering opened at a marked page and showed it to him. "And this!" He opened where another slip of paper had been inserted. "Everything we want to know, practically."

"I don't get this." He wasn't sick, anymore, just bewildered. "I read some reviews of this thing. All the reviewers panned hell out of it—'World War II Through a Bedroom Keyhole'; 'Henty in Black Lace Panties'—that sort of thing."

"Yeh, yeh, sure," Pickering agreed. "But this Hernandez had illusions of being a great serious historical novelist, see. She won't try to write a book till she's put in years of research—actually, about six months' research by a herd of librarians and college-juniors and other such literary coolies—and she boasts that she never yet has been caught in an error of historical background detail.

"Well, this opus is about the old Manhattan Project. The heroine is a sort of super-Mata-Hari, who is, alternately and sometimes simultaneously, in the pay of the Nazis, the Soviets, the Vatican, Chiang Kai-Shek, the Japanese Emperor, and the Jewish International Bankers, and she sleeps with everybody but Joe Stalin and Mao Tse-tung, and of course, she is in on every step of the A-bomb project. She even manages to stow away on the *Enola Gay*, with the help of a general she's spent fifty incandescent pages seducing.

"In order to tool up for this production-job, La Hernandez did her researching just where Lourenco Gomes probably did his—University of Montevideo Library. She even had access to the photostats of the old U.S. data that General Lanningham brought to South America after the debacle in the United States in A.E. 114. Those end-papers are part of the Lanningham stuff. As far as we've been able to check mathematically, everything is strictly authentic and practical. We'll have to run a few more tests on the chemical-explosive charges—we don't have any data on the exact strength of the explosives they used then— and the tampers and detonating device will need to be tested a little. But in about half an hour, we ought to be able to start drawing plans for the case, and as soon as they're finished, we'll rush them to the shipyard foundries for casting."

Von Schlichten handed the book back to Pickering, and sighed deeply. "And I thought everybody here had gone off his rocker," he said. "We will erect, on the ruins of Keegark, a hundred-foot statue of Señorita Hildegarde Hernandez. . . . How did you get onto this?"

Pickering pointed to a young man with dull brick colored hair, who was punching out some kind of a problem on a small computing machine.

"Piet van Reenen, over there, he has a girl-friend whose taste runs to this sort of literary bubble-gum. She told him it was all in a book she'd just read, and showed him. We descended in force on the bookshop and grabbed every copy in stock. We are now running a sort of gaseous-diffusion process, to separate the nuclear physics from the pornography. I must say,

Hildegarde has her biological data very well in hand, too."

"I'll bet she'd have fun writing a novel about these geeks," von Schlichten said. "Well, how soon do you think you can have a bomb ready for us?"

"Casting the cases is going to slow us down the most," Pickering said. "But, even with that, we ought to have one ready in three days, at the most. By two weeks, we'll be turning them out on an assembly-line."

"I hope we don't need more than one. But you'd better produce at least half a dozen. And have some practice-bombs made up, out of concrete or anything, as long as they're the right weight and airfoil and have some way of releasing smoke. Get them done as soon as you have your case designed. We want to be able to make a couple of practice drops."

There was no use, he thought, of raising hopes which might prove premature. He told Paula Quinton, of course, and Themistocles M'zangwe, and, by telecast on sealed beam, King Kankad and Air-Commodore Hargreaves. Beyond that, there was nothing to do but wait, and hope that Hargreaves could keep Orgzild's bombers away from Gongonk Island and Kankad's Town and that Hildegarde Hernandez had been playing fair with her public. He visited the city, where a few pockets of diehard resistance were being liquidated, and where everybody who had not been too deeply and publicly involved in the *znidd suddabit* conspiracy was now coming forward and claiming to have been a lifelong friend of the Terrans and the Company. Von Schlichten returned to Gongonk Island, debating with himself whether to declare a general amnesty or to set up a dozen guillotines in the city and run them around the clock for a week. There were cogent arguments for and against either procedure.

By 2100, the last organized resistance had been wiped out, and curfew had been imposed, and peace of a sort restored. There was still the threat from Keegark, but it was looking less ominous now than it had the evening before. Von Schlichten and Paula were having dinner in the Broadway Room, confident that there was nothing left to do that they could do anything about, when the extension phone that had been plugged in at their table rang.

"Colonel Quinton here," Paula identified herself into it, and listened for a moment. "There has? When?... Well, where did it come from?... I see. And the direction?... Anything else?"

Apparently there was nothing else. She hung up, and turned to von Schlichten.

"The *Sky-Spy* just detected a ship lifting out from Keegark, presumed one of the Boer-class freighters, either the *Jan Smuts* or the *Oom Paul Kruger*. It was first picked up on contragravity at about a hundred feet, rising vertically from near the Palace. The supposition is the geeks had her camouflaged since the time Commander Prinsloo first bombarded Keegark with the *Aldebaran*. That was about twenty minutes ago; at last report, she's fifty miles north of Keegark, headed up the Hoork River."

Von Schlichten started thinking aloud: "That could be a feint, to draw our ships north after her, and leave the approach to Konkrook or Kankad's open, but that would be presuming that they know about the *Sky-Spy*, and I doubt that, though not enough to take chances on. They know we have ground and ship-radar, and they may think they can slip down the Konk Valley either undetected or mistaken for one of our ships from North Uller."

He picked up the phone. "Get me through on tele-cast to Air-Commodore Hargreaves, aboard the *Procyon*," he said. "I'll take it in the office; I'll be up directly." He rose. "Finish your dinner, and have the rest of mine sent up," he told Paula.

Leaving the elevator, he rushed into the big head-quarters room just as contact was established with the *Procyon*, on station over the northwestern corner of Takkad Sea, between Kankad's Town and Keegark. The *Aldebaran*, he knew, was west of Keegark; the *Northern Lights*, now fitted with a pair of 155-mm guns, in addition to her 90's, had just arrived at Kan-kad's. He had the *Aldebaran* sent north along the crest of the mountain-range between the Hoork and Konk river-valleys, where she could cover both with her own radar and other detection-devices and exchange information with the *Sky-Spy*, and the *Gaucho* sent in what looked like the right course to intercept the Boer-class freighter from Keegark. The *Northern Lights*, also with screens tuned to the *Sky-Spy*, was sent to take over the *Aldebaran's* regular station. Finally, he called Skilk and had the *Northern Star* sent south down the Hoork Valley.

After that, there was nothing to do but wait, and watch the screens. Paula Quinton put in an appearance shortly after he had finished calling Skilk, pushing a cocktail-wagon on which their interrupted dinners had been placed. They finished eating, and drank coffee, and smoked. Most of the rest of his staff who were not busy on the bomb-project or at the shipyards or with the occupation of Konkrook drifted in; they all sat and stared from one to another of the screens,

which told, in radar-patterns and direct vision and
telescopic vision and heat and radiation detection, the
story of what was going on to the northeast of them.

Keegark was dark, on the vision-screen; evidently
King Orgzild had invented the blackout, too. Not that
it did him any good; the radar-screen showed the city
clearly, and it was just as clear on the radiation and
heat-screens. The Keegarkan ship was completely
blacked out, but the radiations from her engines and
the distinctive radiation-pattern of her contragravity-
field showed clearly, and there was a speck that marked
her position on the radar-screen. The same position
was marked with a pin-point of light on the vision-
screen—some device on the *Sky-Spy*, synchronized
with the detectors, kept it focused there. The Company
ships and contragravity vehicles all were carrying topside lights, visible only from above, which flashed
alternate red and blue to identify them.

Time crawled slowly around the clock-face on the
wall, the sixty-five-second minutes of Uller dragging
like hours. The spots that marked the enemy ship and
her hunters crawled, too; seen from the hundred-and-
fifty-mile altitude of the *Sky-Spy*, even the six-hundred-
mile speed of the *Gaucho* was barely visible. They
drank coffee till the stuff revolted them; they smoked
until their throats and mouths were dry, they watched
the screens until they thought that they would see them
in their dreams forever. Then the *Gaucho* reported
radar-contact with the Keegarkan ship, which had begun to turn in a hairpin-shaped course and was coming
south down the Konk Valley.

After that, the *Gaucho* began reporting directly,
and her topside identification-light went out.

"... doused our lights; we're down in the valley,
altitude about a thousand feet. We're trying to get a

glimpse of her against the sky," a voice came in. "We're cutting in our forward TV-pickup." The voice repeated, several times, the wavelength, and somebody got an auxiliary screen tuned in. There was nothing visible on it but the darkness of the valley, the star-jeweled sky, and the loom of the East Konk Mountains. "We still can't see her, but we ought to, any moment; radar shows her well above the mountains. Ah, there she is; she just obscured Beta Hydrae V; she's moving toward that big constellation to the east of it, the one they call Finnegan's Goat. Now she'll be right in the center of the screen; we're going straight for her. We're going to try to slow her down till the *Aldebaran* can get here. . . ."

The enemy ship was vaguely visible, now, becoming clearer in the starlight. She was a Boer-class freighter, all right. Probably the *Jan Smuts;* the *Oom Paul Kruger* had last been reported at Bwork, and there was little chance that she had slipped into Keegark since the uprising had started. For all anybody knew, she could have been destroyed in the fighting before the Bwork Residency fell.

"All right, we have her spotted; we're going to open up on her," the voice from the *Gaucho* announced. "She has two 90's to our one; we'll try to disable them, first." The vision-screen lit with the indirect glare of the gun-flash, and the image in it jiggled violently as the ship shook to the recoil, then steadied again, with the enemy ship visible in the middle of it, growing larger and larger as the *Gaucho* rushed toward her. The gun fired again and again, flooding the screen with momentary yellow light and disturbing the image as the recoil shook the gun-cutter. The enemy ship began firing in reply; the shots were all wide misses. Apparently the geek guncrew didn't know how to synchronize the radar sights, and were ignorant of the correct setting for the proximity-fuses. The *Gaucho*'s searchlights came on, bathing her quarry in light. It was the *Jan Smuts;* the name and the figurehead-bust of the old soldier-philosopher were plainly visible. Her forward gun had been knocked out, and she was trying to swing about to get a field of fire for her stern-gun.

"We're going to give her a rocket-salvo," the voice said. "Watch this, now!"

The rockets leaped forward, from the topside racks, four and four and four and four, at half-second intervals. The first four hit the *Smuts* amidships and low, exploding with a flare that grew before it could die away as the second four landed. Nobody ever saw the third and fourth four land. The *Jan Smuts* vanished in a blaze of light that blinded everybody in the room; when they could see again, after some thirty seconds, the screen was dark.

In the direct-vision screen from the *Sky-Spy*, the whole countryside of the Konk Valley, five hundred miles north of Konkrook, was lighted. The heat and radiation detectors were going insane. And in the shifting confusion on the radar-screen, there was no trace either of the *Jan Smuts* or the *Gaucho*.

"Well, the geeks did have an A-bomb," Themistocles M'zangwe said, at length. "I'd been trying to kid myself that we were just preparing against a million-to-one chance. I wonder how many more they have."

"Paula, find out who was in command of the *Gaucho;* he'd be a junior-grade lieutenant. Fix up orders promoting him to navy captain, as of now. It's probably the only thing we can do for him, anymore. And promotions of the same order for everybody else aboard

that cutter. Authority Carlos von Schlichten, acting
Governor-General." He picked up a phone. "Get me
Commander Prinsloo, on *Aldebaran*. . . ."

He ordered Prinsloo to launch airboats and make
a search; cautioned him to be careful of radiation, but
to take no chances on any of the *Gaucho*'s comple-
ment being still alive and in need of help. While that
was going on, the *Sky-Spy* reported another ship coming over her horizon to the east, from the direction of
Bwork. That would be the *Oom Paul Kruger*. Hargreaves had already learned of the advent of the second freighter. He was unwilling to take the *Procyon*
off her station until the *Aldebaran* returned from the
Konk Valley. In this, von Schlichten concurred.

Somebody suggested that a drink would be in order. They had just watched the all-but-certain death
of three Terran officers, fifteen Terran airmen, and
ten Kragans, but they had all been living in too close
companionship with death in the past three days—or
was it three centuries—to be too deeply affected. And
they had also watched, at least for a day or so, the
removal of the threat that had hung over their heads.
And they had seen proof that they had a defense against
King Orgzild's bombs.

They were still mixing cocktails when Pickering
phoned in.

"Some good news, general, from Operation 'Hildegarde.' We ought to have at least one bomb ready to
drop by 1500 tomorrow, four or five more by next
midnight," he said. "We don't need to have cases
cast. We got our dimensions decided, and we find
that there are a lot of big empty liquid-oxygen flasks,
or tanks, rather, at the spaceport, that'll accommodate
everything—fissionables, explosive-charges, tampers, detonator, and all."

"Well, go ahead with it. Make up a few of them; as many as you can between now and 2400 Sunday." He thought for a moment. "Don't waste time on those practice bombs I mentioned. We'll make a practice drop with a live bomb. And don't throw away the design for the cast case. We may need that, later on."

XV -

A Place in my Heart
for Hildegarde

The company fleet hung off Keegark, at fifteen thousand feet, in a belt of calm air just below the seesawing currents from the warming Antarctic and the cooling deserts of the Arctic. There was the *Procyon,* from the bridge of which von Schlichten watched the movements of the other ships and airboats and the distant horizon. The *Aldebaran* was ten miles off, to the west, her metal sheathing glinting the red light of the evening sun. There was the *Northern Star,* down from Skilk, a smaller and more distant twinkle of reflected light to the north of *Aldebaran.* The *Northern Lights* was off to the east, and between her and *Procyon* was a fifth ship; turning the arm-mounted binoculars around, he could just make out, on her bow, the figurehead bust of a man in an ancient tophat and a fringe of chin-beard. She was the *Oom Paul Kruger,* captured by the *Procyon* after a chase across the mountains northeast of Keegark the day before. And, remote from the other ships, to the south, a tiny speck of blue-gray, almost invisible against the sky, and a smaller twinkle of reflected sunlight—a garbage-scow, unflatteringly but somewhat aptly rechristened *Hildegarde Hernandez,* which had been altered as a bomb-carrier, and the gun-cutter *Elmoran.* With the glasses, he could see a bulky cylinder being handled off the scow and loaded onto the improvised bomb-catapult on the *Elmoran*'s stern. Shortly thereafter, the gun-cutter broke loose from the tender and began to approach the fleet.

"General, I must protest against your doing this," Air-Commodore Hargreaves said. "There's simply no sense in it. That bomb can be dropped without your personal supervision aboard, sir, and you're endangering yourself unnecessarily. That infernal-machine hasn't been tested or anything; it might even let go on the catapult when you try to drop it. And we simply can't afford to lose you, now."

"No, what would become of us, if you go out there and blow yourself up with that contraption?" Buhrmann supported him. "My God, I thought Don Quixote was a Spaniard, instead of a German!"

"Argentino," von Schlichten corrected. "And don't try to sell me that Irreplaceable Man line, either. Them M'zangwe can replace me, Hid O'Leary can replace him, Barney Mordkovitz can replace him, and so on down to where you make a second lieutenant out of some sergeant. We've been all over this last evening. Admitted we can't take time for a long string of test-shots, and admitted we have to use an untested weapon; I'm not sending men out under those circumstances and staying here on this ship and watch them blow themselves up. If that bomb's our only hope, it's got to be dropped right, and I'm not going to take a chance on having it dropped by a crew who think they've been sent out on a suicide mission. What happened to the *Gaucho* when she blew the *Smuts* up is too fresh in everybody's mind. But if I, who ordered the mission, accompany it, they'll know I have some confidence that they'll come back alive."

"Well I'm coming along, too, general," Kent Pickering spoke up. "I made the damned thing, and I ought to be along when it's dropped, on the principle that a restaurant-proprietor ought to be seen eating his own food once in a while."

"I still don't see why we couldn't have made at least one test shot, first," Hans Meyerstein, the Banking Cartel man, objected.

"Well, I'll tell you why," Paula Quinton spoke up. "There's a good chance that the geeks don't know we have a bomb of our own. They may believe that it was something invented on Niflheim for mining purposes, and that we haven't realized its military application. There's more than a good chance that the loss of the *Jan Smuts* has temporarily demoralized them. Personally, I believe that both King Orgzild and Prince Gorkrink were aboard her when she blew up. That's something we'll never know, positively, of course. That ship and everything and everybody in her were simply vaporized, and the particles are registering on our geigers now. But I'm as sure as I am of anything about these geeks that one or both of them accompanied her."

"Paula knows what she's talking about," King Kankad jabbered in the Takkad Sea language which they all understood. "Just like Von saying that he has to go on our cutter, to encourage the crew. They always insist that their kings and generals go into battle, particularly if something important is to be done. They think the gods get angry if they don't."

"And we have to hit them now," von Schlichten said. "They still have a couple of bombs left. We haven't been able to locate them with detectors, but those geeks Kankad's men caught on that commando-raid, last night, say that there were at least three of them made. We can't take a chance that some fanatic may load one into an aircar and make a kamikaze-raid on Gongonk Island."

The *Elmoran* ran alongside, with her Masai-warrior figurehead and the black cylinder on her catapult aft. Somebody had painted, on the bomb: DIRE DAWN *by Hildegarde Hernandez. Compliments of the author to H.M. King Orgzild of Keegark.* A canvas-entubed gangway was run out to connect the ship with the cutter. Von Schlichten and Kent Pickering went down the ladder from the bridge, the others accompanying them. As he stepped into the gangway, Paula Quinton fell in behind him.

"Where do you think you're going?" he demanded.

"Along with you," she replied. "I'm your adjutant, I believe."

"You definitely are not going along. Personally, I don't believe there's any danger, but I'm not having you run any unnecessary risks. . . ."

"Von, I don't know much about the way Terrans think, except about fighting and about making things," Kankad told him. "And I don't know anything at all about the kind of Terrans who have young. But I believe this is something important to Paula. Let her go with you, because if you go alone and don't come back, I don't think she will ever be happy again."

He looked at Kankad curiously, wondering, as he had so often before, just what went on inside that lizard-skull. Then he looked at Paula, and, after a moment, he nodded.

"All right, colonel, objection withdrawn," he said.

Aboard the *Elmoran,* they gave the bomb a last-minute inspection and checked the catapult and the bomb-sight, and then went up on the bridge.

"Ready for the bombing mission, sir?" the skipper,

a Lieutenant (j.g.) Morrison, asked.

"Ready if you are, lieutenant. Carry on; we're just passengers."

"Thank you, sir. We'd thought of going in over the city at about five thousand for a target-check, turning when we're halfway back to the mountains, and coming back for our bombing-run at fifteen thousand. Is that all right, sir?"

Von Schlichten nodded. "You're the skipper, lieutenant. You'd better make sure, though, that as soon as the bomb-off signal is flashed, your engineer hits his auxiliary rocket-propulsion button. We want to be about fifteen miles from where that thing goes off."

The lieutenant (j.g.) muttered something that sounded unmilitarily like, "You ain't foolin', brother!"

"No, I'm not," von Schlichten agreed. "I saw the *Jan Smuts* on the TV-screen."

The *Elmoran* pointed her bow, and the long blade of the figurehead warrior's spear, toward Keegark. The city grew out of the ground-mist, a particolored blur at the delta of the dry Hoork River, and then a color-splashed triangle between the river and the bay and the hills on the landward side, and then it took shape, cross-ruled with streets and granulated with buildings. As they came in, von Schlichten, who had approached it from the air many times before, could distinguish the landmarks—the site of King Orgzild's nitroglycerin plant, now a crater surrounded by a quarter-mile radius of ruins; the Residency, another crater since Rodolfo MacKinnon had blown it up under him; the smashed *Christiaan De Wett* at the Company docks; King Orgzild's Palace, fire-stained and with a hole blown in one corner by the *Aldebaran*'s bombs. . . . Then they were past the city and over open country.

"I wish we had some idea where the rest of those bombs are stored, sir," Lieutenant Morrison said. "We don't seem to have gotten anything significant when we flew reconnaissance with the radiation detectors."

"No, about all that was picked up was the main power-plant, and the radiation-escape from there was normal," Pickering agreed. "The bombs themselves wouldn't be detectable, except to the extent that, say, a nuclear-conversion engine for an airboat would be. They probably have them underground, somewhere, well shielded."

"Those prisoners Kankad's commandos dragged in only knew that they were in the city somewhere," von Schlichten considered. "How about midway between the Palace and the Residency for our ground-zero, lieutenant? That looks like the center of the city."

The cutter turned and started back, having risen another ten thousand feet. Morrison passed the word to the bombardier. The city, with the sea beyond it now, came rushing at them, and von Schlichten, standing at the front of the bridge, discovered that he had his arm around Paula's waist and was holding her a little more closely than was military. He made no attempt to release her, however.

"There's nothing to worry about, really," he was assuring her. "Pickering's boys built this thing according to the best principles of engineering, and the stuff they got out of that big-economy-size shilling-shocker all checked mathematically. . . ."

The red light on the bridge flashed, and the inter-com shouted, *"Bomb off!"* He forced Paula down on the bridge deck and crouched beside her.

"Cover your eyes," he warned. "You remember what the flash was like in the screen when the *Jan Smuts* blew up. And we didn't get the worst of it; the pickup on the *Gaucho* was knocked out too soon."

He kept on lecturing her about gamma-rays and
ultraviolet rays and X-rays and cosmic rays, trying to
keep making some sort of intelligent sounds while
they clung together and waited, and, with the other
half of his mind, trying not to think of everything that
could go wrong with that jerry-built improvisation
they had just dumped onto Keegark. If it didn't blow,
and the geeks found it, they'd know that another one
would be along shortly, and . . .

An invisible hand caught the gun-cutter and hurled
her end-over-end, sending von Schlichten and Paula
sprawling at full length on the deck, still clinging to
one another. There was a blast of almost palpable
sound, and a sensation of heat that penetrated even
the airtight superstructure of the *Elmoran*. An instant
later, there was another, and another, similar shock.
Two more bombs had gone off behind them, in Keegark; that meant that they had found King Orgzild's
remaining nuclear armament. There were shattering
sounds of breaking glass, and heavy thumps that told
of structural damage to the cutter, and hoarse shouts,
and lurid cursing as Morrison and his airmen struggled
with the controls. The cutter began losing altitude,
but she was back on a reasonably even keel. Von
Schlichten rose, helping Paula to her feet, and found
that they had been kissing one another passionately.
They were still in each other's arms when the pitching
and rolling of the cutter ceased and somebody tapped
him on the shoulder.

He came out of the embrace and looked around.
It was Lieutenant (j.g.) Morrison.

"What the devil, lieutenant?" he demanded.

"Sorry to interrupt, sir, but we're starting back to
Procyon. And here, you'll want this, I suppose." He

held out a glass disc. "I never expected to see it, but at that it took three A-bombs to blow you loose from your monocle."

"Oh, that?" Von Schlichten took his trademark and set it in his eye. "I didn't lose it," he lied. "I just jettisoned it. Don't you know, lieutenant, that no gentleman ever wears a monocle while he's kissing a lady?"

He looked around. They were at about eight hundred to a thousand feet above the water, with a stiff following wind away from the explosion area. The 90-mm gun, forward, must have been knocked loose and carried away; it was gone, and so was the TV-pickup and the radar. Something, probably the gun, had slammed against the front of the bridge—the metal skeleton was bent in, and the armor-glass had been knocked out. The cutter was vibrating properly, so the contragravity-field had not been disturbed, and her jets were firing.

"It was the second and third bombs that did the damage, sir," Morrison was saying. "We'd have gone through the effects of our own bomb with nothing more than a bad shaking—of course, on contragravity, we're weightless relative to the air-mass, but she was built to stand the winds in the high latitudes. But the two geek bombs caught us off balance. . . ."

"You don't need to apologize, lieutenant. You and your crew behaved splendidly, lieutenant-commander, best traditions, and all that sort of thing. It was a pleasure, commander, hope to be aboard with you again, captain."

They found Kent Pickering at the rear of the bridge, and joined him looking astern. Even von Schlichten, who had seen H-bombs and Bethe-cycle bombs, was impressed. Keegark was completely obliterated under an outward-rolling cloud of smoke and dust that spread out for five miles at the bottom of the towering column.

There had been a hundred and fifty thousand people in that city, even if their faces were the faces of lizards and they had four arms and quartz-speckled skins. What fraction of them were now alive, he could not guess. He had to remind himself that they were the people who had burned Eric Blount and Hendrik Lemoyne alive; that two of the three bombs that had contributed to that column of boiling smoke had been made in Keegark, by Keegarkans, and that, with a few causal factors altered, he was seeing what would have happened to Konkrook. Perhaps every Terran felt a superstitious dread of nuclear energy turned to the purposes of war; small wonder, after what they had done on their own world.

For one thing, he thought grimly, the next geek who picks up the idea of soaking a Terran in thermoconcentrate and setting fire to him will drop it again like a hot potato. And the next geek potentate who tries to organize an anti-Terran conspiracy, or the next crazy caravan-driver who preached *znidd suddabit,* will be lynched on the spot. But this must be the last nuclear bomb used on Uller. . . .

Drunkard's morning-after resolution! he told himself contemptuously. The next time, it will come easier, and easier still the time after that. After you drop the first bomb, there is no turning back, any more than there had been after Hiroshima, four-hundred-and-fifty-odd years ago. Why, he had even been considering just where, against the mountains back of Bwork, he would drop a demonstration bomb as a prelude to a surrender demand.

You either went on to the inevitable catastrophe,

or you realized, in time, that nuclear armament and nationalism cannot exist together on the same planet, and it is easier to banish a habit of thought than a piece of knowledge. Uller was not ready for membership in the Terran Federation; then its people must bow to the Terran Pax. The Kragans would help—as proconsuls, administrators, now, instead of mercenaries. And there must be manned orbital stations, and the Residencies must be moved outside the cities, away from possible blast-areas. And Sid Harrington's idea of encouraging the natives to own their own contragravity-ships must be shelved, for a long time to come. Maybe, in a century or so...

Kankad had a good idea, at that, a most meritorious idea. He was sold on it, already, and he doubted if it would take much salesmanship with Paula, either. Already, she was clinging to his arm with obvious possessiveness. Maybe their grandchildren, and the Kankad of that time, would see Uller a civilized member of the Federation....

They paused, as the gun-cutter nuzzled up to the *Procyon* and the canvas-entubed gangway was run out and made fast, looking back at the fearful thing that had sprouted from where Keegark had been.

"You know," Paula was saying, echoing his earlier thought, "but for that female pornographer, that would have been Konkrook."

He nodded. "Yes. I hope you won't mind, but there will always be a place in my heart for Hildegarde."

Then they turned their backs upon the abomination of Keegark's desolation and went up the gangway together, looking very little like a general and his adjutant.

Turn the Page

For an exciting Sneak Preview of the new
science fiction martial arts adventure,
coming from Ace in August

Streetlethal

by

Steven Barnes

Chapter One

Maxine

Naked and transparent, the woman's pale white body undulated slowly, beckoning to the empty streets. The streets were still slick from the afternoon rain: the hologram reflected back from the wet asphalt, an erotic mirage.

Next to her, impossibly huge, a one-man waterbike revved noisily, churning out ethereal waves of foam. Closer to the deserted streetcorner a shoe the size of a human body moved up and down to its own rhythm, a rectangle above it flashing "Shoe Repair."

Maxine Black laughed at the holo display as she turned the corner. The rain had washed the air clean and she inhaled deeply, savoring the taste. She was a tall woman, broad-shouldered and firm-bodied, who walked with lithe self-assurance. Her eyes remained cool despite her smiling mouth.

As tall as she was, she was dwarfed by the man at her side. He moved as quietly as a shadow, and the arm that gripped her waist possessively was as solid as woven cable.

They passed a blood spectrograph machine—one slot for dollars, one for a Service Mark card. Maxine looked up at her companion playfully. "Ya want to check my B.S., Aubry?" Her voice was throaty and little-girlish at the same time.

His dark, scarred face crinkled in a rare smile.

"You're clean, baby. We checked you two days ago—and you haven't had enough time to get into trouble." His arm tightened on her. "You better keep it that way."

She nuzzled up to him, kissing chin, tiptoeing to kiss lips and run the edge of her tongue into his mouth. "Don't get scary, lover. I won't Spider on you."

They walked through the marching shoe with only a slight flinch as the hologram came down on their heads. The phantom waves splashed by the water-bike brought a smile back to Aubry's face, as if a long-abandoned memory were stirring to life. She pretended to gather a handful of the "foam" and sling it at him. "You shouldn't waste water like that." He laughed, spinning her into his arms for a long, deep kiss. "You make me happy." He shook his massive head in wonder. "I don't know if I've ever said that to anybody." He rolled the words past his lips again, savoring. His eyes were very gentle. He took her hand as they walked through the naked body of the belly dancer. "I'm not used to good things."

"You'd better start, lover. Your life is headed for big changes." There was something in her voice that made him uneasy, and he squinted at her in puzzlement. She felt the tension in the air, and dissolved it with a chuckle. "Good things. You're a contender now, baby."

He nodded, satisfaction and pride replacing the unease. "But I half killed myself for that. Any idiot who can thump heads wants to ride the big rocket, do his thing up there in the clouds." He stopped, looking up in wonder. Barely a handful of stars shone through the overcast night sky. "Nullboxing. I still can't believe I made it."

"You made it because you're good."

"Because fighting is all I know, and they need dudes who don't mind killing each other for money. That's just guts. But you—" His eyes ravished her for the thousandth time. The maddening curves of her body, the face that seemed a Master's collage of ovals and crescents... "You're the only thing that doesn't fit. You just fell into my lap and turned everything around." His low, rough voice almost cracked, and belied his twenty-eight years. "You're the best thing that ever happened to me, and you just fell out of nowhere."

Maxine ran her fingertips over his heavy eyebrows, the puffy rise of his cheeks, down to the fine wire stubble on his chin. She felt her throat constrict. "Let's not talk about it," she said huskily. "Let's just have the night."

She steered him further down the street, past the fluxing, beckoning projections that lined Pacific Coast Highway. Sound loops triggered by their passing cajoled, promising the finest in services and goods; the ultimate in intimate experience. A hungry taxi drone paused on its eternal run down the central guidestrip, and Maxine waved it on.

"Come on," she said, pulling at Aubry. Then she pushed him away and started across the street without him. She made it a race, and he let her get half-way across before he moved. Without preparation of any kind he was moving fast, a fluid streak crossing the yellow pools of light.

Maxine shrieked, laughing, and wasted a moment finding the gate through the low fence that sealed off the beach. Aubry hurdled it effortlessly, slowing his pace as he neared her. He pretended to stumble, *whoofing,* but dove into a roll, springing up to snare her at the waist.

They wrestled for a moment and he went down, Maxine astride him, triumphant and panting in the moonlight. She beat her chest, growling. Gritting his teeth and snarling back he staggered to his feet, her legs still wrapped around his waist. "Jesus you're heavy..." She smothered his words with a kiss and pressed her body to his, twining her legs and arms tightly.

When she pulled her face back there was fire in her eyes, flames that flickered in a cold wind. She peeled herself off and stepped back, reaching out for his hand. "Come on, big man. Let's go bite some moonlight."

The arm he slung around her as they walked was gentler now, warmer. The night breeze was heavy with wet decay, but like true city dwellers they shut that information away, concentrating instead on the echoing roar of the breakers.

The beach was almost totally theirs. Only one lone figure sat quietly in the sand, a dim outline in the pale light.

"I like his attitude," Aubry murmured. "Nothing can stop me from going where I want to go." He shrugged his big shoulders and swung his arms forcefully, then pointed to the rows of highrise office/apartments lining the beachfront. "Damned if I'd live like them. Sitting tight in their cubbyholes, hooking together over their facephones to make their bread. Won't even come out onto the beach except in gangs. Makes me sick."

He dropped his arm around her again as they walked towards the coiling, hissing breakers. The moonlight crested the waves with glittering silver patterns that shattered into darkness on the shore. "Are you cold?"

"Why?"

"I felt you shaking a little, that's all."

She moved closer to him. "Maybe."

"Well, it looks like our friend over there is sitting on a blanket. I bet if we asked him real polite, he'd let us borrow it."

"Aubry . . ."

He smiled evilly.

"You'd better not . . ." she snagged one of his hands, and he pulled her along behind him. She dug in her heels. "Aubry, don't be crazy—"

Aubry was only three paces from the man now. The figure was still immobile, a slender dark silhouette against a silvered backdrop. With elaborate politeness, Aubry addressed the silent one. "Oh, excuse me—"

There was no sound or action, but suddenly something red and hungry was in the air, and Maxine stumbled back.

"Walker?" Aubry whispered. The seated man seemed to unscrew from the ground. Slowly, gracefully, he came to full height facing them. His hands were empty.

"Where is it, Knight?" Walker asked, his voice low and hollow. He was lanky, with arms that seemed disproportionately long. The sinuousness of his rise contradicted his clumsy build. His hair was cut squarely, without style, and in the darkness his eyes seemed wet smears.

Aubry scanned the beach uneasily. "Where's your sleeping buddy?"

"Don't need Diego for this, big man. Don't need nothing but little Loveless."

Aubry's voice shook with tension. "I got no hassle with you."

Walker's laugh was ugly. "That's not what Luis

says . . ." He turned his palms front and back, exposing their emptiness. "C'mon, Knight . . . where is it?" The thin man lunged forward. Aubry jumped back, his heel catching in the sand. Walker laughed nastily. "Maybe I didn't even bring little Loveless."

"You brought it . . ." Aubry's eyes never left the hands of the man who approached him, step light as a dancer's. "But I don't get it. If Luis wants me, why like this?"

"He's a sportin' man, Aubry. You know that. He figures that if you're good enough to walk out on him, you're good enough to deserve a chance. Sportin'." Aubry's stomach grew heavy, then hot as the anger began to build. He forced his breathing to steady, and waited. Walker slid forward a meter, and suddenly his right foot hissed in a short arc.

Aubry pivoted right, and Walker's kick missed his left knee by a centimeter. With phenomenal lightness for so large a man, Aubry continued in a tight circle, spinning a rear thrust kick into Walker that could have broken the man in half.

But Walker was out of range. He snapped his right hand like a lounge magician performing a card trick, and it suddenly held a gleaming spike. A finger moved almost imperceptibly and the six-inch metal tube began to whine.

Aubry backed up again. Loveless Chain-Knife: a flexible razor strip whirred around its edge. It could slice effortlessly through bone. Walker thrust, and Aubry moved to the side, feinting lightly with a kick. There was a quick swirl of motion, and they were out of range again.

"Loveless wants you . . ." Walker said in a hypnotic monotone. The blade made whining criss-cross patterns in the dark. "Ohh . . . don't be mean to Loveless. He just wants to kiss you—"

Before the last syllable was out of his mouth, Walker moved. He seemed to take a single sliding step, but his reach of leg and arm combined to take him much too far into Aubry's defensive space. Aubry parried and dropped to the sand for a leg-sweep that failed, then scrambled back like a crab as Walker lunged. He rolled backwards and sprang to his feet.

Walker paused, grinning, then started in again. Aubry feinted with his left foot—and threw a handful of sand into Walker's eyes.

The thin man screamed, slashing the air in front of him as he retreated. Aubry was on him in an instant, spearing Walker's right knee with a kick. There was a grinding snap as the leg buckled. As Walker fell he back-handed with the knife. Aubry blocked with his right hand, and broke Walker's arm with his knee. As the knife fell from nerveless fingers Aubry twined his fingers in Walker's hair, drawing the head up and back. His hand blurred, and the hard edge slammed down into the trachea. Walker's body slumped face down in the sand.

Aubry panted, kneeling to check the body. "We'd better—" he jerked his head around, eyes narrowed. "Maxine?" There was nothing on the beach, no one, only the sound of the breakers rolling against the earth.

Alarmed now, Aubry jumped to his feet, eyes searching the empty beach. "Maxine!" Fear and uncertainty shook his voice. He ran in a half-circle around Walker's prostrate body.

"Maxine!" Desperate now, he ran towards the highway, towards the distant pools of yellow light.

He was a dark hurricane of movement, but long

before he reached the fence he heard the whirring police skimmers. Their searchlights were glaring white ovals dancing on the sand. He broke hopelessly to the left, then right again in a zig-zag that gained him only a few seconds. Then the skimmers bracketed him, pinioning him in their lights, and the grating-glass sound of their loud-hailers wracked his ears.

"Do not *move*. We are tracking you *now*. Any attempt to initiate hostilities will cause your death. Repeat. We are tracking you *now*." Aubry looked down at his chest and saw the tiny red dot of the targeting laser, and knew that its twin focused on his back. One sudden movement and a burst of hollow-point .22s would rip him into pieces. Numb with the sudden inescapability of it, he lay down on the sand and spread his arms.

Booted feet approached quietly, and a knee pinned him to the ground. A strong arm jerked his own to the small of his back. His wrists were taped together, and he was hauled to his feet. His captors wore the standard dark blue police armor and reflective face shields.

Aubry shut his eyes against the light, and a red roadmap of veins exploded into view. He tried to lower his head, but powerful fingers twined into his hair, pulling him erect.

A man's voice sounded, harsh against the hum of the skimmers. "Is this the man?"

Aubry wet his lips with the tip of his tongue. He growled and tried to shake off the hands, but they held fast. Through the bright wall of pain came the reply: "I couldn't forget a face like that."

Aubry sagged, only the hands at head and shoulders keeping him from sprawling to the ground. "All right, stow this garbage. Get someone downbeach to check the lady's friend. Miss—"

"Black. Maxine Black." Consciousness became a swirl of dark red: Aubry fought to think.

"Miss Black. You understand that the beach is off-limits at night? There will be questions..."

Two faceplated officers hauled Aubry to the waiting skimmer. As he got one foot up on it, he finally left the searchlight's cone of brilliance, and could see the face of his accuser. Maxine gazed at him nervously, then looked away at the ground.

"You!" He screamed in a voice that would have carried at a whisper. "You set me up!" The hands on his back were insistent, but he fought against them in a rage that was close to suicidal.

Their eyes locked. "I'll get you for this. I don't care what it takes. You...and Luis, but especially you, bitch. Do you hear me? *Do you?*"

Her chin lifted slightly, her face tightening. The hands forced him into the skimmer, but he didn't resist this time, keeping his eyes on her as the metallic tape on his wrists was magnetically locked to the restraint bar. He watched her as the skimmer rose whooping from the ground, until she was a tiny vulnerable figure surrounded by uniformed specks.

At the bottom of a tempered crystal flask were two insects. They were fat and pale, greenish-white with a row of vestigial legs along their puffy underbellies. They writhed as Maxine burned them alive.

Her fingers shook as she waved the butane torch under the flask, and she licked her lips. Her tongue was rancid and slimy in her mouth. She watched the dying larvae with eyes that were bloodshot and scratchy. "Please, Aubry. Leave me alone. This time. Please..."

She looked at the anesthetic-steeped tube that had held twelve of the insects, twelve larvae of the South American Coal Moth. Gone now, as these two would be in a moment.

With barely audible pop the first grub burst, and then the second. Vapor from their bodies filled the tube. Maxine clamped her mouth over the top, ignoring the heat, and sucked the vapor into her lungs. It had a harsh minty taste. Whimpering, she sank to the filthy rug of her one-room apartment, and held her breath.

Eyes tightly closed, she could see the light begin to glow in her chest. It crept outward through her blood stream, penetrating her muscles, her bones...

She exhaled in an extended whistle, and let the light spread, the weight of her body and mind lost, driven far away by the drug.

She began to laugh. Just a giggle at first, then hiccoughing hysteria. "All gone. Everything's gone..."

"Your account will be credited..." Luis Ortega told her on the phone, his voice and face so calculatedly pleasant that a sneer would have seemed friendly in comparison.

His face swelled, grew solid and warm, bobbing in the whirlpool of images that filled her mind.

Luis. What a handsome, handsome man, Latino and Chinese, with a full sensuous mouth and a voice to match. A body that sent chills up her spine. She could use a body like that right now. Now, with the heat and light coiling around her like a nest of snakes.

Then Luis wavered, snarled, darkened, and became Aubry Knight.

Knight: his face flayed of all human emotion as

the judge pronounced sentence: fifteen years at hard labor.

His eyes had been a light chocolate brown when she first met him. At the moment of sentencing, through some trick of the light, they seemed the deepest, coldest black that any eyes could be, and they held a vast and certain promise. *We will meet again,* they said, *and when we do....*

And for the first time during the trial, the first time since that terrible night on the beach, Aubry smiled. It was a tight little smile, meant for her and her alone. Then, unresisting, he was led from the courtroom.

Maxine Black sweated and whimpered in her grub dreams, praying for release.

BEST-SELLING
Science Fiction
and
Fantasy

MORE SCIENCE FICTION! ADVENTURE

H.BEAM PIPER
ULLER
UPRISING

ACE SCIENCE FICTION BOOKS
NEW YORK

This Ace Science Fiction Book contains the complete
text of the original hardcover edition.
It has been completely reset in a typeface
designed for easy reading, and was printed
from new film.

ULLER UPRISING
An Ace Science Fiction Book

PRINTING HISTORY
Twayne edition / 1952
Ace edition / June 1983

ISBN: 0-441-84292-5

Ace Science Fiction Books are published
by Charter Communications, Inc.
200 Madison Avenue, New York, New York 10016.
PRINTED IN THE UNITED STATES OF AMERICA